*Two Weirdos
and a Ghost*

YEARLING BOOKS / YOUNG YEARLINGS / YEARLING
CLASSICS are designed especially to entertain and
enlighten young people. Patricia Reilly Giff,
consultant to this series, received her bachelor's
degree from Marymount College and a master's
degree in history from St. John's University. She
holds a Professional Diploma in Reading and a
Doctorate of Humane Letters from Hofstra
University. She was a teacher and reading
consultant for many years, and is the author of
numerous books for young readers.

For a complete listing of all Yearling titles,
write to Dell Readers Service,
P.O. Box 1045, South Holland, IL 60473.

Two Weirdos and a Ghost

PATRICIA WINDSOR

A Yearling Book

Published by
Dell Publishing
a division of
Bantam Doubleday Dell Publishing Group, Inc.
666 Fifth Avenue
New York, New York 10103

The trademark Yearling® is registered in the U.S. Patent and Trademark Office.

The trademark Dell® is registered in the U.S. Patent and Trademark Office.

ISBN: 0-440-40515-7

Printed in the United States of America

October 1991

10 9 8 7 6 5 4 3 2 1

OPM

To Laurence Edward Windsor
the original Teddy Windbag
and
to my friend Marge Lewis

1.

Martha woke up to a rumbling sound outside her bed-room window. Then she heard men's voices shouting to each other. It was a nice sunny morning, the kind that makes you want to jump out of bed. But it was still very early and Martha didn't feel like getting up before she absolutely had to. She stayed under the covers, trying to think what was happening outside. Just maybe, she thought with a shiver of excitement, someone was moving into the old house.

It would be nice not to have all those empty windows staring at her like eyes every time she walked past. New neighbors would be interesting. Maybe they'd have children. Her sister, Jemima, would be ecstatic if they had a boy. She was always saying, "Maybe some neat guy will move in next door."

Finally Martha couldn't stand the suspense and she got out of bed and looked out the window. Sure enough, she could see the long orange roof of a moving van.

Jemima was at the kitchen table when Martha came down for breakfast, doing *he loves me, he loves me not* with the mini–shredded wheats.

"People are moving in next door," Martha told her.

"He loves me not," Jemima said, looking cross-eyed at

her spoon as she popped the last biscuit into her mouth. "See, it's just like I suspected. Mellow is up to something."

"Up to what?" Martha asked. Mellow Rollings had been Jemima's boyfriend for a year and he seemed calm and steady.

"I don't know . . . he's . . ." Jemima jerked her shoulders up and down as she searched for the right words. "He's just so nice but he's acting funny."

Martha tipped the cereal box over her own bowl. All she got was dust. "If you'd had one more biscuit left, it would have come out he loves you," Martha told her. "You can't decide your fate with mini–shredded wheats."

Jemima scowled. "This is a big problem," she said. "You're too young to understand."

"Maybe your problem will soon be over," Martha said as she bent down to search for more cereal in the cabinet.

"Oh, sure, how?" Jemima asked in a bored way.

"I just told you. Next door. A neat guy might be moving in this minute."

Jemima screeched and leapt out of her chair. "Why didn't you say so? Nobody tells me anything." She raced out of the room.

Martha decided just to grab an apple and eat it on her way to school. She wanted to have some time to check out next door, anyway. She'd put on her knapsack and was ready to leave when Mom came in.

"What's all this mess?" Mom asked, eyeing the dishes Jemima had left on the table.

"Jemima. She hogged all the cereal again."

Mom shook her head. "That's the third box this week. I'll have to talk to her."

Martha slipped out the door and went around the side of the house to see what the new people were like.

The long orange van had somehow fit itself into the narrow driveway between the two houses. Its side doors were open and four men in uniforms were carrying boxes up the front steps and through the front door of the old house. Martha didn't see any new people.

"Mind yourself, now," the moving men said, but they didn't tell her to go away. She stayed to watch the boxes going in. But you couldn't tell anything from a bunch of cardboard boxes. She craned her neck to get a look inside the truck.

"Pssst!" a voice hissed behind her. It was Jemima, hiding in the bushes.

"What?" Martha called, and Jemima frowned and shrank back.

"Be quiet, will you? Is he there?"

"Who?"

"The guy!" Jemima whispered. "I don't want him to see me looking like a mess."

Martha noticed that Jemima had changed her hairstyle. At the kitchen table it had been pulled back into a ponytail. Now it was all frizzed out around her face, as if she'd given it a blast with the hair dryer.

"You look all right," Martha said.

Jemima groaned. "You're no help! Is he there or not?"

Martha relented. "There's nobody here but the moving men."

"Oh, for crumb's sake!" Jemima flounced out of the bushes, brushing twigs from her sweater. "You made me late for school."

Martha hung around. She hoped she would see a clue

to what the new people were like. But all that came out of the van were nondescript cardboard boxes. One more load, Martha promised herself, and then I'll go.

She was about to give up when two huge cartons marked FRAGILE CHINA were shifted and something caught her eye, gleaming from the shadows at the back of the truck. It was something tall and golden and somehow familiar. Martha stared, knowing time was ticking away. Then it dawned on her. It was a harp.

A harp seemed very nice. As much as Martha thought new neighbors would be nice, she was also worried about what they would be like. A harp seemed very interesting. Music would come from the house. Happily, Martha hurried to the corner, raced across Bailey Avenue with the light, and galloped the three blocks up Ducktrap Road. She could see Teddy Winterrab's Day-Glo orange anorak like a beacon up ahead. It was just like him to wait.

"Why'd you have that silly smile on your face?" he asked grumpily when she came to a breathless stop.

"I guess because I'm glad. New people are finally moving into the old house next door to us."

"I'm glad too," Teddy said. "I thought I'd be standing here all day. What kind of people?"

"I don't know yet, except for one thing. They have a harp."

Teddy laughed as they pushed through the school's main door. "Maybe they're angels," he said.

Martha laughed too. Miss Hatton, the teacher they hated most, jumped out of the corner and told them to be quiet.

"You just made it," she said, slicing the air with her sharp nose. "The bell is about to ring." She raised a pointy finger and the bell went off. Miss Hatton gave them one of her special grins, showing all her teeth like a skeleton head.

"Another close call with the witch," Teddy said as they slipped into their classroom and took their seats.

Martha agreed. She felt extra lucky to be in Mrs. Ellery's class this year. Mrs. Ellery wore jeans and told them stories about her little boy Pete. She didn't mind when the kids called her Celery behind her back.

Martha got out her workbook and pencil but her mind was on the new people.

"Wouldn't it be wonderful," she whispered to Teddy, "if they turn out to be like Mrs. Ellery?"

"You better hope," Teddy said. "What if you got somebody like the witch?"

Martha's good mood evaporated a little. But then, a person like Miss Hatton would never play the harp.

The house next door had been empty since Martha and her family moved from their apartment to their new house in Melody Woods. From the very first Martha had liked the house and wondered if they'd ever get neighbors. Sometimes, her parents complained about the house, saying it was getting run down. Jemima said it was creepy, but her opinion didn't really count.

To Martha the house was sort of special. She always hoped that whoever moved in would be special too. The harp was a good sign. She just knew it.

2.

That afternoon they had cooking club, so it was already five o'clock when Martha and Ted left school. They walked slowly so they wouldn't unbalance the slabs of cardboard they were carrying. On each slab was half the carrot cake that she and Ted had baked. The cake was covered with sticky cream-cheese icing and the cooking-club teacher had stuck toothpicks into it to keep the waxed paper from mushing it up. A lot of cream cheese was in Martha's hair and under her fingernails. She hoped she'd never have to taste another carrot cake again. She'd joined the club only because Teddy was so enthusiastic. He wanted to learn how to cook properly, since he had to do it for himself so often.

Ted said good-bye at Ducktrap Road. Martha felt sick from licking the batter off the spoon and the cream cheese out of the bowl, but the closer she got to home the more tingly the sick feeling became until by the time she reached Willow Street it had turned into excitement. She hurried up to the old house, then slowed down. The cake almost fell off the slab and she had to stop to make an adjustment. It was a good opportunity to peek at the house, to see if the new people were hanging around. The moving truck had gone and all the boxes were inside. But the house still looked empty. The only change was a withered plant in a red pot left on one of the porch steps.

Martha went up the driveway, hoping to see some signs of life, but the windows were dark and still uncurtained. She went in through her kitchen door.

"Here," she said, dumping the cardboard slab onto the kitchen table. "I brought dessert."

Martha's mom eyed the cake suspiciously. Mom was basically against sweets, especially if they contained any bad ingredients.

"It's all pure," Martha told her. "We had to grate a million carrots."

Mom put her finger out and picked off a dab of icing. "Sugar, Martha!" she said. "I bet there's a ton of it in this."

"Jemima will eat it," Martha said. She wasn't interested in the cake. She wanted some news. But her mother went back to making black marks all over some printed pages she'd brought home from her office. She was a reporter for the local newspaper and wrote stories about things that were happening all over town. Martha liked to see the finished blocks of print with *by Betsy Lewis* under the title. Sometimes her mom took photographs to go with her stories.

"Did you see them yet?" Martha asked.

"Who?" her mom said, frowning at the words she was reading.

"The new people."

"The new people?"

Martha felt exasperated. "The people who moved in next door!"

Mom looked up and tapped the pencil eraser against her chin. "Well," she said. "Well. No, not really."

It was hard to believe a mother could be so uninterested. Martha started to tell her about the harp but she could see Mom wasn't listening.

"Marth, go upstairs and wash that awful gunk out of your hair, whatever it is," she said distractedly.

"It's only cream cheese. Listen, I—"

"I have to get these galleys done tonight," Mom said.

Martha sighed. As she was climbing the stairs, Dad came in the front door. "Hi, sweetheart," he said. "What happened to your head?"

"Cream cheese." She was going to tell him about the new people, but Mom came into the hall and started talking.

"You won't believe it," she said. "Those people did buy it."

"I was worried about that," Dad said gloomily. "I'd been hoping the deal would fall through. What we don't need is crazy people living next door."

"Maybe it will be all right," Mom said.

"Not from what I've heard about them," Dad said. He looked up and saw Martha sitting at the top of the stairs. Mom did too. "Martha! Didn't I tell you to wash your hair? Do it now so there will be enough hot water for the dishwasher after dinner."

It wasn't really her hair, Martha knew. They just didn't want her to hear. They'd said crazy people had bought the house next door. Would crazy people play the harp?

It was no use trying to get more information at dinner. Jemima did *he loves me, he loves me not* with her peas, Dad talked about the office, and Mom talked about the newspaper. Mom served the carrot cake for dessert. Dad said it was delicious. Jemima only smelled it and said she was on a diet.

"You'd better cut down on cereal," Mom suggested. "You're getting too much bulk."

This made Jemima burst into tears. She ran away from the table, leaving Martha to help with the dishes on her own again. "It's not fair," Martha said, but Mom explained that Jemima was going through a difficult stage.

"I'm going through a stage that makes it difficult for me to do all Jemima's work," Martha said, but she helped anyway. Being in the kitchen alone with Mom was a good opportunity to get information. But Mom still didn't want to talk about it. She said she'd seen some people going in and coming out again, but that's all.

At bedtime Martha turned out her light early and looked across at the house. The windows looked back, like blind eyes. The only light that showed was downstairs, a yellowish glow on the porch. I guess they're out, Martha thought. But at least it's nice to have the house waiting for someone to come home to again.

Crazy people didn't necessarily have to be bad. Only misunderstood. A lot of the kids at school called Teddy Winterrab crazy. They also called him Teddy Windbag because he talked so much. But Martha was used to him now and she knew he wasn't really weird. Only different.

She turned over in bed and felt better. Probably the new people were like Teddy, a little offbeat and different. That's why they played the harp. One thing was for sure: They were definitely going to be interesting, just as she'd hoped.

9

3.

On Saturday morning Martha woke up very early. Not because she wanted to but because of the screeching that was going on under her bedroom window.

"Fitz! Max! Bud! Suze!"

Well, that's one normal thing, Martha thought. The people next door had dogs. She jumped out of bed and hurried over to the window to see what kind. Down below, a tall woman in a strange red dress like a tent was walking down the driveway. No sign of the dogs. Maybe they'd run off. Maybe they'd run back to their former house. Dogs sometimes did that. Martha had wanted a dog when they moved to Melody Woods. Pets had not been allowed at the Grape Hill Apartments. But Mom said it wasn't fair, there'd be no one home all day. So instead they got a cat, Margaret. Margaret didn't like being home alone all day either and was usually at someone else's house.

Martha pulled on her jeans and T-shirt and ran downstairs. Harvey Bender was in the kitchen, sitting at the table slurping milk and cereal. Most of it was on the table or on him.

"What's he doing here?" Martha asked.

"I'm baby-sitting," Jemima said. She was sitting across

from Harvey, staring at a slice of unbuttered toast. "I hate this diet," she added.

"I think you look fine," Martha said.

Harvey slipped off his chair and went under the table. Martha dragged a stool over to the counter to eat her breakfast there. "Are you going to hang around here with him all day?" she asked Jemima.

Jemima shrugged, got up, and opened the refrigerator. She took out the margarine and a jar of homemade strawberry jam. "The heck with it," she said, scooping big gobs of jam onto the toast. "Nope. Mellow is taking us to the park."

"I thought you were off Mellow," Martha said.

Jemima ignored her.

"I suppose last night's peas said he loves you, huh?"

Jemima was about to throw a toast crust when Dad came in. Dad always slept late on Saturdays. "Catching up," he called it. He looked sleepy and a little grumpy. He sat down at the table and began to drum his fingernails.

"That woman," he said. "I hope she's not going to make a habit of screaming every Saturday morning."

"I think she was calling her dogs," Martha said, pouring him some coffee from the automatic coffee maker.

"It was six A.M.!" Dad said.

Martha waited until Dad blew on his coffee to cool it and took a few sips. He always said he wasn't human until he'd had his coffee in the morning. Mom didn't approve of drinking coffee, but she gave in. It wouldn't be any good having a husband who wasn't human, she said.

"Dad," Martha asked when he had downed half a cup.

11

"Don't you think we should bring something over to the people next door?"

Dad shook his head. "It's a nice idea, Marth. But I'm not so sure . . ."

"It's the neighborly thing to do," Martha said.

"You're right," Dad agreed. "But I don't feel very neighborly this morning."

Martha was getting exactly nowhere. "What's their name, do you know?" she asked.

"Rose," Dad replied. "Mr. and Mrs. Rose."

"Do they have any . . . um . . . kids or anything?" Jemima asked.

"Not that I know of," Dad said.

Jemima threw Martha a look. Martha shrugged. It was too bad there wouldn't be a neat guy next door.

"But now you tell me they have dogs," Dad said wearily. "We'll be overrun." Then he gave a yelp. "Something bit me!" He pulled his legs out from underneath the table. "What's under there?"

"It's only Harvey," Martha said.

"Come out, you brat," Jemima scolded.

"I'm going back to bed," Dad said. He took his coffee mug and limped out of the kitchen.

"Well, I guess I can forget about next door," Jemima said.

Martha was disappointed in her family. Dad always said to give a guy a chance. And Mom was always lecturing on how it was bad to listen to gossip. But here they were, listening to gossip about the neighbors being crazy. And all Jemima cared about was neat guys.

Martha decided she had to get the facts. She'd make a visit to the Roses and decide for herself.

12

The phone rang and Jemima ran to get it first. Martha was left alone in the kitchen with the mess and Harvey. He peered out from under the table and made a disgusting noise. Martha made a horrible face back at him. Harvey began to scream. Jemima came rushing back in. "What's the matter now?"

"She scared me," Harvey wailed.

"What a big baby," Martha said.

"He's only a little kid," Jemima said, trying to pull Harvey out to give him a hug. He kicked and pushed and got his snotty nose all over her sweatshirt. "Ugh, you are a baby," Jemima yelled at him. Martha had to help her wipe the snot off with a wet sponge.

"Thanks," Jemima said. "Ooops, I forgot. The phone call's for you."

"Sorry," Martha said when she picked up the receiver, but Teddy was already talking before the word was out of her mouth.

"My mother's mad at me," he said. "I'm in big trouble. I had to come out to call you on the pay phone at the 7-Eleven."

"What's up?"

"I found this dog."

"What dog?"

"A dog. He latched on to me when I was walking up Bailey Avenue. He followed me and he seemed so nice, so I brought him home."

"You should notify the owner," Martha said. "What does his collar say?"

"He has no collar. I mean, he has a flea collar and a nice blue leather collar, but no tags."

"That proves he's not a stray." Martha pondered a

moment. "You know Ted, maybe I can help. I think I might know where the dog came from."

"You do?" Teddy sounded shocked. "How could you know that?"

"It's just a chance," Martha said, and told him how the woman next door had been calling her dogs early that morning.

"I'm really sorry to hear that," Teddy said. "It's only marginally better than the pound. My mother said I had to bring him to the pound. I begged to keep him but she's like you, she said he wasn't a stray and the owners would be looking for him and it was only fair I brought him to where they'd find him." Teddy paused. "The truth is, I don't really want to find the owner. I'm getting to like this dog. I want to keep him."

"That's not fair, is it?" Martha said. "And anyway, your mother said you couldn't."

"Well, she didn't say that exactly. She said that if no owner claimed him during the ten-day waiting period at the pound, she might reconsider."

"So what's the big trouble you were talking about? It looks like everything's under control."

"Except for one thing. I need a place to keep him until the ten days are up."

Martha had to take a deep breath. "You have a place to keep him, the dog pound."

"I couldn't do that," Teddy shrieked into the phone. "You know what those places are like. Who says they'll wait ten days? They could gas him by mistake or some phony person could come in and say he's the owner. No way am I bringing this dog to a dangerous place like the pound."

"But, Teddy, think of the real owner. Don't you think he'll be worried about his dog?"

"I have thought," Teddy said reluctantly. "And I decided I would put up notices on telephone poles and stuff. Maybe your mom would give me an ad in the newspaper free, do you think?"

Martha didn't really want to get involved. Getting involved with Teddy's schemes could bring a lot of trouble. "Listen, before you do anything, let me check with the people next door. Maybe the dog belongs to them."

"Gee, Marth, I didn't think calling you would lead to this. What if the dog ran away from home because he was miserable? I mean, those people could have been rotten and cruel and maybe he couldn't stand it anymore."

"Not you too?" Martha said angrily.

"Not me too what?"

"Starting in on the people next door. First my parents accuse them of being crazy and now you say they're cruel. You don't even know them."

"I was just theorizing, Marth. . . ."

"If the dog is theirs, you'd better be prepared to bring him right over," Martha said sternly.

"Why are you so mad?"

"I'm hanging up now," Martha said. "I'll call you back with the news."

"I can't hang out here all day."

"At home, I mean. You'd better be there, and no tricks."

She banged the phone down and spent a moment trying to catch her breath. Then she opened the front door for Mellow Rollings. He was all dressed up in his best clean jeans and a blinding white shirt. His hair was still a little damp from washing it. He didn't look like he was up to anything.

Harvey had to make a couple of fusses before he was ready to go. Dad called down to complain about the noise. Finally, Jemima, Mellow, and Harvey left. Martha found some shiny apples and fairly new grapes in the refrigerator. She put them in one of Mom's bread baskets and called up to Dad that she was leaving too.

"Peace and quiet at last," Dad said.

Martha let herself out the door and walked across the driveway to the old house.

4.

She'd been on the porch before but she'd never knocked at the door. The old brass knocker made a hollow booming sound inside the hall. Martha waited. She wondered if she should knock again. Then she heard a rustling sound and the door opened. The woman in the strange red dress peered out.

"Yes?"

"I'm Martha Lewis from next door," Martha said. "Welcome to the neighborhood." She held out the basket of fruit. The grapes looked a little dusty in the sunlight.

"How downright nice," the woman exclaimed, opening the door wider. "Your mother is real thoughtful. Would you like to come in?"

Martha nodded, biting her tongue to keep from saying the fruit was her idea, not her mother's. She stepped over the threshold into the cool, shadowy hall. It was a lot different from her house; older and darker and full of carved wood banisters and wood panels halfway up the walls. There was a gigantic mirror that seemed to go right up to the ceiling. All along its edges were hooks. Martha guessed they were for people's hats. But who would own so many hats? And how could you get them down from the ceiling?

The woman's red dress swished around her as she walked. She led Martha through a big archway into a living room. There were boxes piled all over, reminding Martha of how her own living room had looked when they were getting ready to move from Grape Hill Apartments. A couple of chairs stood in the center of the room.

"Sit yourself down," the woman said. "And excuse the mess. We're still all of a doodah here."

Martha sat down in one of the chairs and the woman sat in the other. She smiled in a friendly way. She was a little older than Martha's mother and very thin, and she didn't look crazy. But she talked a little funny. Maybe she came from one of those places way out in the country where there wasn't much civilization, Martha thought. Her dad called it the boondocks.

"Now tell me every little thing about yourself," the woman said, but when Martha opened her mouth to speak, she kept right on talking. "We're the Roses here. I'm Flora Rose and my husband is Harcourt Rose. We call him Harky for short. He's gone down to the shops on an errand but he'll be back any moment. I know he'll want to meet you. And we'll be looking forward to meeting all the rest of your family. Now tell me every little thing about them."

Martha didn't think that was such a good idea. She changed the subject and asked about the dogs. She might as well find out as quickly as possible if one of them had run away.

"Dogs, honey?" Mrs. Rose asked, looking puzzled.

"I heard you calling them this morning," Martha said.

"You did? Now, that's a funny thing. I don't recall any dogs this morning. We used to have a nice dog but he got old and we put him down. That was a long time ago." Mrs. Rose tapped her head with a long, skinny finger. "No, I can't say I saw any dogs this morning." She peered at Martha with glittery eyes. "Did you see them?"

Martha changed the subject again, so Mrs. Rose wouldn't have to feel so puzzled. She probably forgot. Martha's grandma had a friend who was almost a hundred and she forgot things. Mrs. Rose didn't look a hundred, though. Maybe, just maybe, she was a little weird. It was okay, of course. Weird could be very interesting.

"This is a real old house, isn't it?" Martha said.

"Why do you ask?" Mrs. Rose said, and her face turned very serious.

It looked like this was the wrong thing to talk about too. "Well," Martha said—why had she ever wanted to be neighborly?—"well, it's not like my house. I mean, it's got all this . . . stuff." Martha pointed to the ceiling, which was covered in carvings like rippling white ribbons. In the center was a round cluster of flowers with a glass chandelier hanging down.

Mrs. Rose looked up at where Martha was pointing. "Now, look at that," she said. "It's very dirty. Every little piece of glass will have to be washed. What a lot of work!"

Martha nodded sympathetically. Mrs. Rose kept staring at the chandelier. Martha wondered how soon she could say she had to leave. She was trying to think of a convincing excuse when the front door opened and a gray-haired man walked in, carrying two grocery bags.

"Harky!" Mrs. Rose cried, sounding a bit like Jemima when she got excited. Mr. Rose came into the room and stopped when he saw Martha.

"This is our little neighbor," Mrs. Rose explained. "She brought us a basket of fruit."

"That's a right nice thing, little lady," Mr. Rose said.

Martha relaxed. Mr. Rose seemed normal.

"But, Harky, listen to this puzzlement," Mrs. Rose said. "Little Martha thinks she saw some dogs around the house this morning."

Mr. Rose looked shocked. "Not dogs too!" he cried. He put the grocery bags down on one of the unpacked boxes. He came over to Martha and looked down at her. "Can you tell us exactly what kinds of dogs you saw?"

Martha gulped. "I didn't really see them. I mean, I heard Mrs. Rose calling them."

The Roses looked at each other and back at Martha. "You did?" they said, sounding alarmed.

"What I mean is . . . I heard . . . well, it was like this," and Martha imitated Mrs. Rose: "Fitz! Max! Bud! Suze!"

There was a horrible silence in the room for a moment. Both Mr. and Mrs. Rose had their mouths hanging open. And then they began to laugh. Mrs. Rose laughed so hard, tears rolled down her cheeks. Mr. Rose put his hand on a box to get his balance and almost fell over anyway.

"You don't know how good it is to hear that," he said.

"Music to our ears," Mrs. Rose agreed.

Martha just sat there.

"I think we'd better explain," Mr. Rose said, recovering. Mrs. Rose wiped her eyes and nodded.

"Those weren't dogs, my dear, they were our children."

"Children?" Martha began to say. How awful! She'd mixed up the Roses' children with dogs.

"They were only here for the night," Mrs. Rose continued. "To help us settle in. They had to leave early this morning."

"They didn't want to go," Mr. Rose said. "They were afraid we couldn't manage on our own after what happened. But Momma hustled them out. You must have heard her calling them to hurry up."

"Gosh, I'm sorry," Martha said.

"No need to apologize, dear," said Mrs. Rose. "They do have doggie names."

Martha smiled a little at that and Mrs. Rose smiled back, and Martha felt one hundred percent better. It had been a misunderstanding and now it was cleared up. The Roses were perfectly normal people. Not crazy at all, but certainly a little interesting.

They walked her to the door. Martha saw the harp standing in the corner and wished she had asked them to play it. She felt very warm and happy now.

"I like this old house," she told them.

They stopped smiling and looked serious again.

"We do, too, dear," Mrs. Rose said quietly. "But there's only the one thing."

Mr. Rose made a move as if to shush her but she put her hand up. "It's all right. Little Martha looks like a sensible girl." Then, to Martha, she said in a whisper, "The trouble is, we don't know if we can stay."

"Oh," Martha said and she guessed her disappointment showed. "But—" she said, wondering if she could ask to hear the harp before they moved out.

"Because," said Mrs. Rose, "you see, the house is haunted."

5.

"A haunted house sounds like a fun idea," said Teddy as he and Martha watched the stray dog run around sniffing trees in Martha's backyard. Teddy was in a great mood because Martha had told him about her visit to the Roses and how the dog was not theirs.

"Maybe we could hide him in their house," he suggested. "They'd just think he was a ghost." He laughed in his windbag way but Martha didn't think it was funny.

"You don't understand," she said, sounding like Jemima. "The house might not be haunted. They could be imagining things because they're . . . uh . . . crazy."

"All the more reason they might agree about the dog."

"Can't you get off that subject?" Martha asked.

"It's a very important subject," Teddy said more soberly. "Because if I don't find a place to keep him, I'll have to take him to the pound."

"Which is where he *should* be taken," Martha said, although halfheartedly. She'd agreed to Teddy bringing the dog over for the afternoon. She wasn't doing much, and she wanted to avoid the moment when Mom met the Roses and Mrs. Rose blabbed about how nice she had been to send over the fruit.

Martha had to admit the dog was special. He was the

only dog she'd ever seen who smiled. He had long black and white hair and droopy ears. He had looked up at her face when she said hello, just as if he could understand. Then he had jumped up, planted his front paws on Martha's shoulders, and given her a big slobbery kiss. Martha's heart had melted. She began trying to think how they could find him a home for the ten-day waiting period that Teddy called "probation."

"But," she said now, "you have to think about the owner's feelings. Someone could be pining away for him."

Teddy didn't want to discuss that. Martha knew he wanted to think the dog had run away from home on purpose, to escape bad treatment.

Teddy found a stick and threw it. The dog fetched and brought it back. "Good boy!" Teddy said, and the dog wagged its tail.

"He needs a name," Martha said. "We can't keep calling him 'the dog' or 'boy.' "

"Yes, only he probably already has a name and he might get confused."

"True," said Martha. The dog watched them as they talked, looking from one face to another as if he understood every word they were saying. He lifted a paw and placed it on Martha's knee.

"Want to tell me your name?" Martha asked.

The dog made a quizzical face. Something happened to his mouth, as if his cheeks had blown up with air. That is, if a dog had cheeks. It was like he was amused and questioning.

Teddy noticed too. "He's teasing," Teddy said. "But

maybe he'd like a new name. You know, to start over and forget bad memories."

"Ted," Martha said again. "It could be that his owners loved him very much."

Teddy frowned and for a moment seemed perturbed. Then his face cleared. "Oh, yeah? Then how come he's so happy? If it was such a nice home, he'd be pining away too."

Martha thought about it. "It's like Harvey Bender," she said. "He's real happy when he's away from home, when Jemima baby-sits him here. But his parents love him. We wouldn't want to keep Harvey."

"Nobody with any brains would want to keep Harvey," said Teddy. "He's a world-class brat."

Martha thought it was a nasty thing to say, but she really couldn't disagree. So she went back to watching the dog run around. It really was nice to live in a private house and have a big backyard and a pet. It was too bad that Margaret the cat didn't like it very much. Maybe what Teddy had said was the truth. Margaret always ran away to someone else's house because she was unhappy staying at home alone. Maybe the dog had the same kind of life and just got fed up. Dad said people had a breaking point. After that it was no telling what they would do. Dad's breaking point was when Jemima was five minutes late getting home from a date with Mellow.

"Listen, Ted, I was thinking maybe you're right—" Martha began to say, but her voice was drowned out by a loud screech from the yard next door.

"Coooooeeeee! Hi, there!" It was Mrs. Rose, calling and waving.

"Is that her?" Teddy whispered. "The crazy woman?"

25

"Shhh," Martha said.

"Hi," Teddy called back to Mrs. Rose. He waved. Mrs. Rose came over to the fence between the two yards. On her side the grass didn't look as nice. It was brown in some spots and long and weedy in others.

"Are you little Martha's brother?" Mrs. Rose asked. She was still wearing the strange red dress.

"I'm a friend," Teddy said, and he went over to the fence and shook Mrs. Rose's hand. She beamed at him. Martha hoped he wasn't going to say something awful about her being crazy.

"I hear you have a problem," Teddy said, sounding exactly like a doctor.

Mrs. Rose cocked her head to the side. "A problem?"

Teddy moved closer so he could whisper conspiratorially into Mrs. Rose's ear. "Something about ghosts, I heard?"

Martha was furious. She was going to murder him. She got up and marched over, ready to apologize to Mrs. Rose. But Mrs. Rose wasn't at all upset. Instead she began to talk to Teddy in earnest, just as if he really were a doctor. She told him how they had been so happy to buy the old house and how they had moved in with the help of Fitz, Max, Bud, and Suze. "Those are my children," she explained to Teddy, "not my dogs." She winked at Martha and Martha knew it was all right.

"We all went to bed early, you see, we were dead tired after the move," Mrs. Rose said. "And that's when it happened."

"What exactly?" Teddy asked.

Mrs. Rose put her hand to her head. "Horrible sounds at first. Harky thought it was the pipes. It woke everybody up. We were all in the upstairs hall in our pajamas and we saw it."

"What exactly did you see?" Teddy asked. Martha thought he should have a stethoscope around his neck.

Mrs. Rose looked at Teddy, then at Martha, as if she was thinking whether they would get scared and act like babies. Martha thought about last year when she and Teddy had done a lot of experiments with a Ouija board, trying to contact the spirits, and how a real spirit did appear in her room once. It had been a little hair-raising, but not absolutely awful. She put on a brave look so that Mrs. Rose would know she could take it, whatever was going to be said.

"An apparition," Mrs. Rose breathed.

"A what?" Martha asked.

"A ghost," Teddy said in his pompous voice.

"I'm afraid so," Mrs. Rose said sadly. "And now we'll have to leave this nice house that took so long to find." She sounded as if she was going to burst into tears.

"Ghosts aren't all bad," Teddy said firmly. He gave Martha a look.

"That's right, Mrs. Rose," Martha said. "Ghosts can be . . . well . . . sort . . . of . . . fun."

Mrs. Rose looked unsure.

"And helpful," Teddy added. "Definitely helpful."

Mrs. Rose gave the kind of smile adults give kids when they think they don't know what they're talking about. "That's a nice thought, honey, but in this case I don't think so."

Teddy had noticed the look and heard the tone in Mrs. Rose's voice. "Look, it's true," he said. "I know from personal experience."

27

"You know about ghosts?"

Teddy grinned and stuck out his chest. He pushed his glasses up on his nose and looked important. "Absolutely," he said. "Martha and I know all about ghosts."

Martha was glad she was finally included, but she wondered if they should be telling all this to Mrs. Rose. The Ouija-board spirit had seemed fun enough and had given them some helpful messages. But they had never actually seen an apparition. Martha looked over at the windows of the old house and a chill crept up her spine. She had always thought of the windows as sad eyes. Now they suddenly seemed to be staring at her in a scary way.

"Listen, Ted," she said, wishing she could get him to shut up. But he kept going on and on, just like an old Teddy Windbag.

"So I have an idea," he was telling Mrs. Rose. "We could help you get rid of the ghost, and then you wouldn't have to move."

Mrs. Rose's face brightened up. "Do you really think you could?"

"Sure thing," Teddy said.

Martha gave him a kick in the ankle, but he brushed her away as if she were a pesky fly.

Mrs. Rose became gloomy again. "But I don't know. It could be dangerous. I wouldn't want anything to happen to you and little Martha."

Martha couldn't have agreed more. What would happen was that Mom and Dad would find out. They'd be really mad.

"Oh, it's perfectly safe," Teddy said. "And since we won't be around, nothing could possibly happen to us."

Mrs. Rose didn't understand. If they weren't going to be around, how could they chase away the ghost?

"Him," Teddy said, pointing to the dog.

As if the dog knew he was being talked about, he stopped sniffing trees and came trotting over. He sat down at Teddy's feet and looked up at Mrs. Rose. His long pink tongue was hanging out.

Mrs. Rose looked down at the dog. "Him?" she asked.

Teddy nodded up and down and his glasses almost slid off his nose.

"The best ghostbuster around!"

Martha groaned and everybody looked at her, including the dog.

"Sorry," she said.

Teddy ignored her. He told Mrs. Rose that if she kept the dog in her haunted house, the ghost would leave. Guaranteed.

"How long do you think it will take?" Mrs. Rose asked.

"Ten days," Teddy said. "Don't worry, we'll bring his dog food and stuff around tonight. You don't have to do anything except keep him in your yard in the daytime and in your house at night."

Mrs. Rose bent down to pat the dog through the fence. "He's very nice," she said. "What did you say his name was?"

Teddy looked at Martha, but she refused to help.

"Er . . . Buster, of course," Teddy said, laughing nervously.

"Well, come along, Buster," Mrs. Rose said. "You might as well start your job now."

She opened the gate at the end of the yard and called the dog in. The dog looked once over his shoulder at

Martha and Teddy and then, as if making up his mind on his own, trotted after Mrs. Rose.

"Teddy Winterrab, you really are the pits! How could you do it?" Martha whispered angrily.

"What's the big deal?" Teddy asked.

"It's a trick, that's what's the big deal. You lied."

"But, Marth," he pleaded. "You said yourself there wasn't any ghost. If they're crazy enough to imagine ghosts, they can be crazy enough to believe Buster will chase the ghosts away."

"Buster is a stupid name!" Martha hissed.

"It was the best I could think of on the spot," said Teddy. "You should have helped."

Martha turned around and stomped back to her house. Teddy followed.

"Are you really mad, Marth? Look at it this way. Now the poor dog has a home for the ten days' probation. It's a lot better than the pound."

Martha marched into the kitchen and opened the refrigerator. She took out a container of juice and poured herself a big glass. She didn't pour one for Teddy. She drank the juice down in a couple of big gulps. Then she felt calmer.

"You forgot one thing, Ted," she said. "If there really is a ghost, it could get us into big trouble."

Teddy didn't say anything. He looked a little mixed up.

"Ghosts aren't so bad, I suppose," she said, not feeling so angry anymore. "And Buster looks like he can take care of himself."

Teddy relaxed. He got a glass down from the cabinet and poured himself some juice. "Good, that's settled. What should we do now?"

"What do you think?" Martha replied. "We go buy a bag of dog food and a couple of chewy bones."

"Okay, little Martha," Teddy said, smiling.

Martha gave him a good punch.

6.

Martha woke up in the middle of the night, certain she had heard a dog howling. It was a spooky sound. She hoped it wasn't Buster. He'd scare the Roses more than the ghost and they'd probably kick him out.

When she woke up again, it was early morning. There was a sound of doors slamming and loud voices under her window. Martha got up and looked out. The Roses were packing their car with suitcases. She wondered if they were kidnapping Buster.

"I think that's all, Harky," she heard Mrs. Rose say. Mr. Rose got into the car, but Mrs. Rose began walking toward Martha's kitchen door. Martha ran downstairs without even putting on her slippers or robe. She got there just as Mrs. Rose banged the knocker.

"Oh, hello, dear," Mrs. Rose said, looking a little startled when the door opened so suddenly. "How nice, you're an early riser. I wanted to give you this and ask if you wouldn't mind looking after Buster while we're away. We had a bad night, you see." She looked over her shoulder at the old house. "We thought it best if Buster does his job alone. We'll come back when it's over. Ten days your little friend said, I think?"

She handed Martha a long white envelope. Behind her

Martha heard people coming down the stairs. "Sure," she said quickly, and began to close the door on Mrs. Rose.

"You're a good little girl, Martha."

"No problem," Martha said, and shut the door. Just in time, too, because the whole contingent came into the kitchen. They all looked grouchy. Mom was frowning and Dad had his eyebrows up on the top of his head and Jemima's face looked like a prune.

"What on earth is going on?" Mom said.

"Is there no peace?" Dad asked, looking sourly at the automatic coffee maker, which hadn't made the coffee yet.

"It's those crazy old bats next door," Jemima reported, looking out the window as the Rose car drove off. "I heard one of their dogs howling last night. It gave me the creeps."

"I knew they'd be trouble," Dad said.

Mom was looking at the envelope in Martha's hand. "What did they want?"

"Oh, they just asked me to take care of their dog while they were away, that's all."

"That's all!" Dad roared. "What a nerve! Banging on the door at seven thirty on a Sunday morning."

Mom turned the switch on the coffee maker and suggested they all sit down. She'd whip up some wheatmeal pancakes, seeing as how nobody was in the mood to go back to bed. Jemima fell into a chair and groaned. Dad kept his eye on the coffeepot. Mom turned to Martha. "You don't have to do it," she said. "It wasn't fair to ask a favor so abruptly."

"It's okay," Martha said. She had opened the envelope and was looking at its contents.

"But it's not really your responsibility," Mom said, pouring milk and eggs into a bowl.

"I don't mind, really," Martha said. "And anyway, Teddy can help, since it is his responsibility."

"Teddy?" they all asked. "What's he got to do with it?"

"Er . . ." Martha said. "He owes me a couple of favors."

"It's not right," Dad said. "I'm going to talk to them as soon as they come back. They're taking advantage of you, Martha."

"But they left me twenty dollars," Martha said, holding out the crisp green bill.

Jemima screeched. "No fair! They should have asked me. An older person can do a better job."

Mom laughed. The smell of coffee began to fill the kitchen, and after a moment Dad laughed too. Only Jemima stayed grumpy. She said she couldn't eat any pancakes because of her diet. But she picked the blueberries out of her serving and did *he loves me, he loves me not* with them all over her plate. Mom said it was disgusting and Jemima ran off in a huff.

Dad heard the thump of the Sunday paper being thrown at their front door. He took his coffee and said he would go read in bed.

When Mom and Martha were alone in the kitchen, Mom asked, "You really don't mind?"

"No, Mom. Honestly, they're okay people."

Mom looked at her quizzically. Martha hurried to explain. "I took them some grapes yesterday. You and Dad were all mad at them before they even had a chance."

34

She was afraid Mom would get mad and tell her the grapes were for dessert or something, but Mom just sat there thinking. Finally, she said, "Well, Martha. I think you've taught us all a lesson."

Martha felt really good inside. Until Mom asked her to help clean up.

"How come Jemima and Dad never have to help?"

"Jemima's going through a stage and Dad helps when he can. But he gets bogged down with so many business problems on his mind."

"How come you don't?" Martha asked. "You have a job now too. And how about me? Nobody asks if I have school problems on my mind. Maybe I'm going through a stage too. Maybe I've just got into a stage of not wanting to help."

Mom laughed. "I don't think so, Marth. You're just too full of natural kindness. I believe you would have looked after the Roses' dog even if they hadn't paid you twenty dollars."

You don't know the half of it, Martha thought. This was definitely a case where natural kindness was causing nothing but a lot of unnatural trouble.

After the kitchen was cleaned, Martha read a book until it was a civilized hour to call Teddy.

"I've got bad news," she told him when he answered the phone.

"You're not kidding. It was a flop. Why is it I can never make a chocolate cake? This time, I forgot to put in the sugar. I was—"

"The dog," Martha interrupted.

"He didn't run away, did he?" Teddy asked in a worried voice.

"No, but the Roses did."

Martha explained. Teddy said everything was cool and not to worry. They could take turns. He promised to come every afternoon after school. And wasn't it great they had twenty dollars to spend?

"*I* have twenty dollars," Martha said. She was turning over a new leaf and giving up kindness.

"But, Marth, it's only fair we split it, if I'm going to help."

"It's my commission," Martha told him. Dad had explained to her once how a person got a commission if he acted as a go-between for one business and another. She certainly had been a go-between for Teddy and the Roses.

"And anyway," she said, "everything is not cool. We have a problem. We'd better find out if there really is a ghost and we'd better do something about it before the ten days are up."

There was a moment of silence. Then Teddy said, "Poor Buster. I hope he won't be scared staying there all alone. This calls for drastic action, Marth."

"I'm glad you agree. What do we do?"

There was another silence. Then Teddy said in a small voice, "Gee, Marth, I don't know. What do you think?"

Martha looked up at the ceiling the way Jemima did when she thought people were acting stupid.

"Go to the library right after school tomorrow," she said, "and get some books on how to negotiate with ghosts."

"Negotiate?" Teddy asked. "That seems a funny thing to do."

"It's a business problem," Martha said firmly. "So we have to do things in a businesslike way."

Teddy got excited. "Gosh, this could be the start of something big. There are probably lots of haunted houses that need our services."

"Could be," Martha said, feeling pleased. It was a good feeling to be a businessperson in business. It had a lot of advantages besides making money. The next time Mom asked her to help with the dishes, Martha was going to say she couldn't. Because she was bogged down by all her business problems. Just like Dad.

"But in the meantime," she added before Teddy hung up, "make sure you come over today to help feed Buster."

7.

There was a good chance she might never wish for anything again. When a wish came true, it wasn't always the way you imagined. She had wished for interesting people to move into the house next door and the result was more kooky than interesting.

It had seemed like a good idea to start a business as ghost chasers, but now that Martha was standing on the Roses' front porch, ready to start the job, she felt like changing her mind.

In the envelope with the note and the twenty dollars, Mrs. Rose had left the keys. Teddy had said he'd be right over, but it took him two hours to arrive. Probably held up by another of his cake disasters, Martha thought sourly. It was raining, only adding to the creepy feeling that had come over her. It was strange. Before, when the house was empty, with big staring windows and no lights, it had seemed perfectly nice. Now that people were in it, with furniture and all, it was suddenly sinister. In a minute she was going to start screeching like Jemima. She gave herself a shake and was relieved to see Teddy coming down the street in his bright orange anorak.

"It's about time," she said in a grouchy voice.

"I had to do two loads of wash," Teddy said. "I had no

38

clean shirts and no clean underwear and no clean socks and—"

"Spare me the gory details," Martha interrupted. She had the key ready in her hand and even the key looked creepy. It was old and rusty. Just like a key to a haunted house should look.

"Gosh, Marth, what's up with you?" Teddy asked.

"Nothing," she said. She marched to the door and stuck the key into the lock before she could change her mind.

"Ha ha," Teddy said behind her. "You know what? I think you're scared, Marth."

"Of course I'm not scared."

"Well," Teddy said, his voice becoming quiet as he looked around, "it is a bit weird." He was looking up at the big mirror that Martha had noticed before. Only, she hadn't noticed that all the leaves and flowers carved around it had faces looking out.

"Ugh," she said, and pulled him away. "Where the heck is Buster?" she asked, suddenly worried.

"He must be around somewhere," Teddy said. He began to call but there was no response. "At least I hope he's around," Teddy added.

"Buster isn't his name, anyway," Martha said. "No wonder he's not answering."

They found Buster behind the closed kitchen door. He jumped on them the minute they opened it, giving big sloppy licks and wagging the whole back half of his body and his little stub of a tail. Then he sat down and looked at them, as if to ask: What next? They found the bag of dog food in the corner. Mrs. Rose had placed two mixing bowls on the floor. One of them was filled with water.

"Want some dinner, boy?" Teddy was asking. Buster wagged his stub and almost seemed to nod his head.

"I think he's already had dinner," Martha said, inspecting the second bowl. It looked as if it had been licked clean very recently. "Mrs. Rose probably fed him before she left."

"Well, a second helping won't hurt," Teddy said. "He needs his strength if he's going to chase ghosts."

Buster had been listening. He agreed by making a low purring sound in his throat. He watched very carefully as Teddy put two cups of dry dog food into the bowl. He waited as Teddy poured on some water.

"Okay, boy," said Teddy. But Buster didn't move. Instead, he looked up at Martha.

Martha looked back at him. She could tell from the gleam in Buster's eye that he knew he was taking advantage by getting two dinners.

"Well, all right," she said. Buster gave her a soft woof and went to the bowl. In a moment he was crunching happily.

"So what should we do first?" Martha said as she sat down at the kitchen table. The Rose kitchen was very different from the kitchen in her house, which was all sparkly with new appliances and white countertops. This kitchen was old, with a big ugly sink with two faucets, one for hot and one for cold, and a refrigerator with a round motor on top. The cupboards were tall and gloomy and there were all sorts of doors leading into unknown and possibly spooky places.

Typical, Martha thought. It was exactly like the kind of kitchen they'd put in a movie about a haunted house.

Suddenly, the refrigerator motor coughed. Buster

looked up from his dish, ears pricked. Then, satisfied that it was nothing important, he went back to eating.

At least he's on the ball, Martha thought. It was comforting to have a dog with them. Animals could sense things that humans couldn't see or hear.

Teddy was busy snooping in the refrigerator. "Nothing much in here," he said, and began searching the cupboards.

"That's rude," Martha said. "We should be deciding on our strategy."

"But this is really strange, Marth. They don't have any real food. Only bottles of water and bags of brown pellets. What do you think? Maybe they're Martians."

"More likely health-food nuts," Martha said, recognizing the brown pellets as the bran buds her mother bought at the health-food store.

Teddy was disappointed. He shut the cupboards and sat down across from Martha and drummed his fingers on the table.

"We have enough problems without Martians," Martha said. "Did you forget about the ghost?"

"Nope," Teddy said. "I was stalling for time, hoping for a cookie break."

"We can have oatmeal cookies later. Give Buster a quick run in the yard and then let's get started on our job."

Buster ran out to do his business, keeping a beady eye on them the whole time, as if afraid they would lock him out. No chance of that, Martha thought. She was counting on him to warn them if a ghost should happen to appear.

When Buster finished, they started on their ghost

search. Teddy was a lot more nervous than he wanted to admit. Martha knew because he began one of his windbag speeches.

"See all those plaster designs around the ceiling at the tops of the walls?" he intoned in a teacher-voice. "It's called Lincrusta. People used to gunk up their houses with it. If it falls off and hits you on the head, you could get a concussion."

He acted like he was directing a tour, telling Martha the correct names for all the old stuff. He said the lights on the walls were called sconces and the staircase railing was a balustrade. "That sounds a lot more glamorous, doesn't it?" he asked, running his hand over the smooth brown wood. Martha didn't tell him to shut up. His babbling was comforting.

There was a feeling in the house. It wasn't something she could describe, just a funny prickle at the back of her neck and a tingle in her stomach.

Maybe it was just her imagination. Mom always said you could get carried away by your imagination. Like when Jemima said she had crooked hair and no boy would ever ask her for a date. Or when a pipe started dripping in Grandma's basement and she phoned up and said her whole house was getting flooded. "It's just your imagination," Mom told them. Or when Martha said Jenny liked Phyllis Blott better because Phyllis had a house, a pool, and two cats and a dog. "You're imagining it," Mom had said. Mom was right most of the time. Jemima did get asked for dates and Grandma's house hadn't flooded. But Mom had been wrong about Jenny.

Martha hoped it was just her imagination now. The trouble was, Buster was acting just the way Martha felt.

The hair on the back of his neck was standing up. Every once in a while his stomach gave a rumble.

Teddy finally stopped talking. They were at the top of the stairs in the upper hall.

"I'm not getting any radiations," he said.

"How do we know ghosts give out radiations?" She didn't tell him she was feeling plenty of radiations herself.

"Well, look, Buster can't even smell them. He's not sniffing around at all."

"Maybe ghosts don't smell."

"Nope. The Roses are crazy, just like your dad said." Teddy's face looked smug and satisfied. "Problem solved."

"Problem not solved," Martha said. "Even if the Roses are the nuttiest people in the world, they still *think* they saw a ghost. And if they did, they'll probably see it again. So they'll know the dog isn't a ghostbuster after all."

Teddy started to protest.

"And we'll have to give back the twenty dollars."

"Why? We're going to take care of him for ten days, aren't we?"

"Under false pretenses," Martha reminded him.

Buster was sitting down between them, watching them talk. Martha wished he could say something.

And, just like before, her wish came true. Buster suddenly lifted his head, opened his mouth, and let out the scariest, most mournful howl Martha had ever heard, better than any horror movie.

8.

Teddy's face looked like a pot of school paste. "Yech! Let's get out of here."

"No, wait," Martha said. She heard something now. The thing that Buster had heard. And she saw that his hair wasn't standing on end anymore. Buster looked happy. His pink tongue was hanging out of the side of his mouth and his head was cocked, ears listening. He seemed to be enjoying the sound.

The harp. The harp was playing somewhere downstairs.

"Oh, rattlesnakes!" Teddy said, and started clomping down the staircase. Halfway down, he slipped and slid the rest of the way on his back.

Martha couldn't help it, she laughed. The prickles on her neck had stopped prickling. The drifting sound of the harp was lovely. She and Buster weren't scared anymore.

"That's real nice," Teddy said, rubbing his back. "Laugh in the face of disaster."

"You should have held on to the *balustrade*," Martha said.

Teddy gave her a glare.

The music stopped. A soft glow was coming from the

living room. They watched it, not wanting to break the spell. Teddy felt it now too. Something warm and possibly friendly was in the house with them.

There was a last ping on the harp and the light went out.

In the silence only Buster's soft panting could be heard. Then Teddy said, "Well, at least we know one thing. It's a good ghost. A bad ghost certainly wouldn't play the harp."

"Let's take a look," Martha said, clumping down the stairs with Buster galloping beside her.

The living room looked perfectly ordinary. There were no more sounds and no more lights.

"Hello?" Martha called out.

"Anybody here?" Teddy said.

Buster gave a soft questioning woof.

There was no answer.

"So much for negotiating with ghosts," Teddy said. "Let's go, I'm dying for a cookie."

"Wait," said Martha. "We have to try. The ghost could still be here listening."

Teddy sat down on one of the unpacked boxes and took off his glasses. They were all sweated up with his excitement and falling down the stairs and he polished them on the end of his shirt.

Martha cleared her throat. She felt a little silly. How did you bargain with a ghost?

"Ahem," she began. "I guess you're a pretty nice ghost and you play the harp good too."

Teddy groaned but Martha shushed him. It was best to tell people good things before you told them bad things. That's what Mrs. Ellery always did when you got a bad mark on a test. First she told you how proud she was of the way you tried. Then she dropped the bomb.

"If you wouldn't mind, could you haunt some other house?" Martha said. "You're scaring Mr. and Mrs. Rose and I'd like them to stay here. This old house has been empty a long time and it's nice to have neighbors. But they won't stay if you keep scaring them. So, if it isn't too much trouble—"

A sudden breeze stirred in the living-room air. It made a little whooshing sound.

"It's here," Martha whispered to Teddy, and he nodded.

Buster looked puzzled. His ears went up and the hair on his back got all frizzy the way Jemima's did when she blasted it with the dryer.

"Woof?" Buster said. He began sniffing along the floorboards.

The breeze sped around the room, picking up momentum, shaking lampshades and rattling Mrs. Rose's knicknacks. As it passed by, it blew Martha's hair into her face. She coughed and spit it out. The glasses Teddy had just pushed back up his nose suddenly slid down again.

"Wait a minute!" Teddy said indignantly. "Let's at least talk!"

The breeze became a wind and the chandelier swayed back and forth, making a horrible creaking sound.

"We've come as friends," Martha said, afraid the chandelier was going to crash. "Really. We only want to negotiate!"

Buster barked. The harp strings gave a great twang and the breeze stopped as quickly as it had started.

"Phew," Martha said.

"You'd better do some fast talking," Teddy said. "This ghost has a temper."

But Martha wasn't sure what to say. She'd already asked politely if the ghost would go away, and she'd seen the answer.

"Er . . . do you think . . . if you stayed here, would you mind leaving the Roses alone? I mean, not appearing to them?"

Instantly, the room was rattling and shaking again, and Martha's hair was blown every which way.

"Okay, okay, it was just an idea!" Martha felt a little angry. It was hard enough trying to talk to something that could only answer with a lot of wind. She didn't need her hair messed up with every word.

Buster didn't like it either. He bared his teeth and growled. And for some reason the wind stopped and all became calm and silent.

"Did you see that!" Teddy exclaimed. "Good boy, Buster. What did I tell you, Marth? He can really do the job, can't he?"

But Teddy's big grin disappeared when the harp began playing again. It wasn't very pretty music either. Just a big twanging and hideous jangling.

Buster immediately lifted his head and howled, which only added to the din.

"Let's get out of here," Teddy shouted.

Martha was mad now. The ghost was acting like a spoiled brat, throwing a fit and refusing to listen to reason.

"Come on," Teddy said, holding his ears. But Martha shook her head and held her ground.

Finally, the noise stopped.

"Finished now?" Martha asked in a fierce voice like Miss Hatton, the teacher they hated most.

An itsy-bitsy ping sounded on the harp.

"Good. Well, we've listened to you, now you listen to us. If you don't stop on all this nonsense, you know what will happen, don't you? The Roses will leave." The harp began to twang again, as if the ghost didn't care what the Roses did.

She'd have to think of something better . . . something a ghost wouldn't like. What could it be? Then it came to her. Ghosts and houses went together. Ghosts had their own houses to haunt and probably wouldn't like moving. "What will happen," Martha said loudly, above the twang, "is that the Roses will leave and the house will be torn down. And then where will you be, huh?"

The harp was dead silent.

"Gee, Marth, that was great," said Teddy.

Martha smiled. Buster wagged his stubby tail. And then all the doors in the house started slamming at once. Martha and Teddy ran to the front door. Buster looked up at them and then at the harp. Clearly, he was undecided.

"Come on, boy," Teddy called from the porch, holding the door open.

Buster shook his floppy ears. He refused to come outside. He lay down across the front doorstep and put his furry black face and shiny black nose on top of his white paws. His big brown eyes looked up at them. He looked adorable—as if he'd gone to cute school, Martha thought.

"I guess he's made up his mind," Martha said.

"He sure looks cute, doesn't he?" Teddy asked.

"He's doing it on purpose," she replied. "But at least you won't have to worry where to keep him. He seems to like it here."

"Which just proves my theory," Teddy said. "The ghost is benevolent."

"Benevolent?"

Teddy gave a teacherish scowl from behind his glasses. "It means kind and good."

"I thought benevolent meant when you gave something, like a quarter for the starving-children collection at school."

"Whatever," Teddy said huffily. "You have to admit it's not a bad ghost."

"Bad or good is not the problem," Martha reminded him. "How do we get rid of it?"

"I need a cookie break," Teddy said.

9.

Sunday night, two things happened. Both of them turned out horrible. The first thing was that Margaret the cat decided to come home for a visit. Martha was really glad to see her and gave her a big hug. It was nice to cuddle Margaret's soft furry body. She smelled good, too, of autumn leaves and fresh cold air. But Margaret took one big sniff of Martha's doggy-smelling sweater and jeans and arched her back, gave a few spits, and ran away again.

The second thing was that Phyllis Blott's mother called. She wanted to know if Phyllis could sleep over on Tuesday night.

"No way!" Martha told Mom. Mom looked surprised. She wanted to know why.

"I'm not friends with The Blot," Martha said. How could she be friends with a person who once stole her best friend and had teeth like a vampire?

"But she's in your class," said Mom. "Her parents have to go out of town to visit a sick relative. I think we can be neighborly for one night, don't you?"

Martha was trapped. She knew Mom was reminding her about how she'd insisted they all be neighborly to the

Roses next door. If she could be neighborly to them, then she'd have to be neighborly to the Blotts.

"Phyllis lives only a block away," Mom said. "It would be nice if you and she became friends."

"No, it wouldn't," Martha said, but it didn't make any difference. Once adults decided things between themselves, there was nothing you could do to change their minds.

This was even more awful than dealing with a ghost. It ruined Martha's whole evening. She didn't enjoy her favorite TV show and she couldn't concentrate on getting her schoolwork together for the next day. All she could think of was having The Blot in her house, in her bedroom! What would they talk about? She pictured them sitting there, staring at each other.

"You sure look mopey," Jemima observed when Martha came out of the bathroom after brushing her teeth. Jemima gave Martha a poke. "Having a little boyfriend trouble?"

"Everybody doesn't think like you do!" Martha snapped.

"Excuse me for living," Jemima said, looking hurt.

"Sorry. I have problems."

Jemima sighed. "Me too. It's too bad you're not old enough to give advice."

"How old is old enough?"

"Well . . . at least my age," Jemima said.

"Good. Then you can give me some advice. What do you do when you have to have a vampire sleeping in the same room as you?"

"For crumb's sake!" Jemima shrieked. "Quit joking around. My problems are *serious.*"

"So are mine," Martha said, and explained about The Blot, who had vampire teeth and was coming to stay the night.

For a change Jemima looked sympathetic. She came into Martha's room and flopped down on the bed.

"The best thing," she said, "is to plan it all out. Don't leave anything to chance and don't leave one single minute empty."

"Plan what?" Martha asked.

"Games, for instance. Listen, I know it sounds corny, but what do you care? Get out all your board games and tell this Blob that you're going to play them all."

"Blot," said Martha. "It's not a bad idea. I have at least ten board games in my closet." She started to feel a lot better. It would serve The Blot right. They'd start with Chutes and Ladders and work all the way through to Monopoly.

"Plan the snacks too," Jemima went on, hugging herself and really getting into it. "Make some nasty cookies. Ask Mom for some of her health-food recipes. Guaranteed to gross you out!" They both fell all over the bed laughing. Then Jemima put on a serious face and changed her tone. "Maybe I shouldn't be encouraging you," she said. "I mean, it's not really nice. This poor Blob is going to come here, all innocent—"

"She's not innocent!" Martha interrupted. "She stole my best friend, Jenny, last year."

"Oh. That's different. That's sort of like my problem. I mean, almost. My best friend is trying to steal my best friend."

Jemima's eyes got teary. Martha waited. Jemima sniffed, then grabbed a tissue and gave her nose a loud blow. She told Martha how her best girlfriend, Denise, was trying to steal her boyfriend, Mellow.

"But Mellow likes you best," Martha said. If Mellow could put up with taking Harvey Bender along on a date, it had to be true love.

"Maybe he does, maybe he doesn't," Jemima said, sounding like when she did *he loves me, he loves me not* with her peas. "It's very complicated."

Martha agreed. People were complicated. They all had their own peculiar reasons for doing things. Like Teddy being afraid to take Buster to the pound, and Mrs. Blott not sending The Blot to Jenny's, and the Roses running away from the ghost. Although that wasn't really peculiar, since Martha wouldn't have liked to spend time with that bad-tempered spirit herself.

"I'd like to fix that Denise good," Jemima was saying.

"Me too," said Martha. "Fix Phyllis, I mean."

"But I can't invite Denise over to play board games, can I?" Jemima wailed. She went over to Martha's mirror to check out her pimples. "I'd have to do something massive to scare her off."

Martha felt the same way. She had to scare Phyllis Blott off. Otherwise, Mom would insist they become friends and start inviting her over for milk and cookies after school. The Blot would start borrowing all her stuff, just the way she tried to borrow all her pens and pencils at school. One day she even tried to borrow lunch. It was too horrible to think of living the rest of her life being friends with The Blot. Martha gave herself a shake and looked out the window. Across the way the Rose house sat, dark and secret. She hoped Buster was doing okay. Maybe the ghost would take the hint and leave.

On the other hand . . . "I might have an idea," Martha said.

"Mmmmm? Like what?" Jemima said, doing a contortion with her head so she could see underneath her chin.

"Like how we can scare them off . . . Denise and The Blot."

Jemima stopped picking at her face and came back to the bed. "So tell," she said.

"Okay, it's like this." Martha explained about the ghost. It took a lot of work. It wasn't easy to convince Jemima that a ghost actually did exist. But finally, she agreed it would be the greatest trick to play on their enemies.

They spent so much time concocting a plan, and talked so loud, that Mom came upstairs. She opened the door and stood there, looking at them.

"I was going to scold you two for staying up so late," Mom said. "But it's wonderful to see you girls getting along so lovingly . . . like sisters should." She beamed a big smile at them. Jemima and Martha smiled at each other.

" 'Night, sis," Jemima said.

"Yeah, sis," said Martha.

"What a pleasant change," said Mom.

Martha snuggled down under the covers. It was funny. Just a couple of hours ago she had been dreading The Blot's visit. Now she couldn't wait.

10.

"I don't approve," Teddy said at lunch the next day at school. He paused in the middle of stuffing his face with a peanut-butter-and-banana sandwich. "It will only cause problems, not solve them."

Martha groaned. She really needed his help in scaring Denise and The Blot. "We're only trying to get back at our enemies a little bit."

"Listen, Marth," Teddy said earnestly. "Making people feel bad only backfires. You end up making yourself feel worse."

"Honestly, you sound just like a parent."

Teddy looked insulted. "I thought of it all by myself! My mother never tells me stuff like that."

"Whatever. But stop lecturing. It's going to be a joke."

Teddy chewed his sandwich and slurped his milk. Martha could see he was getting into one of his windbag moods. He would deliver an all-day lecture if you let him get started.

"Look over there." Martha pointed to the table where Phyllis Blott sat with Martha's former friend Jenny and some other girls. "She's ignoring me, as usual," Martha observed. "She never tries to be friendly, even when she borrows something. She's just plain rude. But tomorrow night she'll be sleeping in my room."

"Hmmmm," Teddy said.

"Do you approve of that?"

Teddy scratched his nose. He took off his glasses, polished them on a paper napkin, and pushed them back on again. "Well. No."

"So, will you help?"

He made a big deal of folding his aluminum foil into squares and squashing down his empty milk cartons. "The Blot isn't *my* enemy. And I don't even know your sister's friend Denise."

"And I didn't know your stray dog," Martha said. "Or open my mouth when you were fooling Mrs. Rose."

Teddy's face went all red and sticky-looking. "That's blackmail!" he cried.

Martha's stomach felt queasy. She wished he would want to help, not have to be forced into it. "Listen, maybe we can make a combo deal," she told him. "We'll scare The Blot and Denise and figure out how to get rid of the ghost at the same time."

"If Phyllis and Denise are as bad as you say they are, the ghost might run away on its own."

"Good. That's settled. We'll go to the library right after school to do some research."

"Don't forget about Buster," Teddy said.

"We'll be home in time to take care of him too."

The bell rang. Lunch period was over. They collected up their stuff to go back to Mrs. Ellery's class.

"Thanks, Ted," Martha said as they slipped into their seats. But she could see that he still disapproved.

They had to read a story about a sly fox and a red hen

in reading group that afternoon. The fox kept trying to catch the hen and she kept getting away. The fox couldn't stand it. He didn't really need to catch the hen, but he kept trying because she made him so mad with her scolding and teasing. One day he thought up a great plan and caught the hen and stuffed her into a bag. But when he finally brought her home and let her out, it turned out to be not as much fun as he thought. The hen looked all scared and sad and she started cleaning up his fox den because it was so dirty. Finally, the fox felt sad, too, and decided he couldn't eat the hen after all.

"Why do you think the fox felt so bad?" Mrs. Ellery asked.

Nobody answered. Everybody looked around, trying to think whether or not they should raise their hands and risk saying something dumb. Martha could feel Teddy's eyes staring at her across the reading circle. She knew what he was thinking. It was just her luck they had to get into this kind of discussion today.

"Doesn't anyone have an idea?" Mrs. Ellery asked.

Teddy raised his hand.

"The fox only caught the hen because he was mad at her, not because he was starved or anything."

"That's a good thought, Ted," Mrs. Ellery said. "Anyone want to comment on what Ted has said?"

Phyllis Blott was sitting next to Martha, breathing on her. She smelled like salami. She raised her hand.

"That fox was a dope," Phyllis said, looking straight at Teddy. "He should've jammed the hen in a pot of boiling water!"

"That's gross," Teddy exclaimed, and suddenly a whole bunch of kids were talking at once. Some were on

Ted's side, some were on The Blot's side. Some said the fox was only acting natural, like a fox should. Others said the hen was a busybody, cleaning up another person's house.

Mrs. Ellery let everybody talk and shout for a while. She said she was glad they were having a discussion and sharing opinions. When they all calmed down, Ted raised his hand again.

"Who was right?" he wanted to know.

"There is no one right answer," Mrs. Ellery replied. "It's what the story means to each of you personally that counts."

Teddy jumped around in his seat impatiently. "But who won the argument?" he asked again.

"This wasn't a contest, Ted," Mrs. Ellery said, and shushed him.

"Ha!" said Phyllis, real loud. "That tells you, Teddy Windbag!

"He's a real weirdo," she said to Martha, more quietly.

"Take a hike, salami breath," Martha told her. She wondered how Teddy felt about giving The Blot a good scare now.

11.

They couldn't find any books that gave quick and easy directions for getting rid of a ghost. Some of the books in the library said you had to find out who the ghost was and ask why it was hanging around. Then you had to solve the ghost's problems so that it would cooperate and leave the house it was haunting.

"Sort of like a ghost psychiatrist," said Teddy.

"It sounds too complicated," Martha said. "I don't think we can do it in ten days."

"Only nine left," Teddy reminded her.

They checked out a couple of the books to take home. Then they had to stop at the Rose house to feed Buster.

It was quiet inside the house. The long, slanting rays of afternoon sun came through the windows and made the rooms seem golden. It didn't feel scary at all.

Buster wagged his tail and hung his pink tongue out the side of his mouth. Martha scratched him behind the ears and he fell over on the floor like a lump and put his legs in the air.

"Buster, stop acting corny," Teddy scolded.

"He's enjoying himself. He's probably lonely."

"Yeah. Maybe the ghost disappeared on its own,"

Teddy said, looking around. "It all seems pretty normal in here."

"What a dirty trick," Martha exclaimed. Now what would she do about scaring The Blot and Denise?

"Or maybe it's just having a nap or something. Listen, I have to hurry and get home to cook dinner. My mom has a meeting on Monday nights and I always cook her spaghetti before she leaves."

While Teddy filled Buster's bowls with food and water, Martha wandered into the living room. The harp was silent. The air undisturbed. Could the ghost have really gone?

"Hello?" she asked the empty room.

"What are you doing!?" Teddy whispered furiously from the hall.

"Just testing."

"Well, don't get into any big discussions now, will you? I told you I had to get out of here."

Martha stayed to listen for a few more moments anyway. But there was absolutely nothing. She was worried. Nice as it was to have solved Mr. and Mrs. Rose's problem, it was going to spoil all the fun tomorrow night. At least the ghost could have stayed until then.

They let Buster out into the yard and locked the door behind them. Martha would come back over after dinner to put Buster back inside for the night.

"Don't forget to call me," she reminded Teddy. "We need to plan our strategy. It may be only a false alarm and the ghost will be back."

"You mean like a lull before the storm," Teddy said, looking back at the windows of the Rose house. "To tell the truth, I hope it is gone."

Well, it would make things easier, Martha supposed. Still, they had to see. Ted waved and went off down the driveway. Martha walked across the yard to her own kitchen door. The kitchen was dark and nothing was on the stove cooking for dinner yet. From upstairs she could hear the muffled booms of Jemima's stereo.

Martha looked around to see if there was a note from Mom about getting dinner started, when Mom came running in the door. She dumped her purse and briefcase onto the kitchen table and heaved a big sigh.

"It's so late! I was out on an interview. Be a good girl, Marth, and wash the salad while I change my clothes."

Martha looked at the ceiling, in the direction of Jemima's music. She considered suggesting that Jemima could come down to make the salad. But then, Jemima would do *he loves me, he loves me not* with every lettuce leaf and radish. Martha heaved a big sigh like Mom's and turned the water on in the sink.

Mom hung up her coat and ran upstairs to put on jeans and a sweater. By the time she came down, Martha had the salad arranged in a wooden bowl.

"Terrific," Mom said. "Now let's see. Some tofu and chicken . . ."

"Being it's so late," Martha ventured, "maybe we could just have burgers?"

Mom's face got the horrified look it always did whenever anyone mentioned unhealthy things like potato chips, taco chips, or french fries.

"Just asking," Martha said.

Mom took the chicken out of the freezer and put the package into the microwave. She pushed the programming buttons. "You know," she said, "I was in a real old-

61

fashioned kitchen today, way over on Pineapple Street. I interviewed a wonderful old lady who still makes soup from scratch."

Martha had a vision of the little red hen scratching around the sly fox's kitchen. "How do you do that?" she asked.

"With a big pot, chicken bones, vegetables, and herbs." Mom said. "It's really sad, though. The old lady lives all alone and her only companion was her dog. That's why we're going to run a big story in the newspaper. Maybe it will help."

Martha got out the silverware and began to set the table. She liked hearing Mom tell stories about her job. "Help how?" she asked, hoping to keep Mom talking. It hypnotized her and gave her a warm, cozy feeling.

"Help find the dog, of course," Mom said.

Martha dropped one of the forks. "The dog?"

"The old lady's dog. She couldn't take it for a walk anymore because she's a little unsteady on her feet and the dog pulled too much. So she used to let him out in the garden. And he ran away." Mom frowned. "Or somebody stole him. You can't tell these days."

Martha picked up the fork and rinsed it at the sink. "What kind of dog was it?"

"Some kind of sheepdog, I think. We'll be running a picture. I have it in my briefcase. I have to write the story tonight so we can get it into Wednesday's edition."

Plenty of people lost dogs, Martha thought. Dogs were running away every minute. Just like cats. Look at Margaret. She was never home. It could be any dog. Buster didn't look like a sheepdog, anyway. Sheepdogs were big and bushy and carried casks under their chins to save people in the mountains. Or maybe that was St. Bernards.

"I'd like to see the picture," Martha said.

"Sure," Mom replied. She started cutting tofu into chunks.

"Could I see it now?"

"What for? Here, help me get this tofu stirred into the sauce."

Martha was going to insist, but Dad came home and Mom began to tell him the story of the old lady all over again. The story sounded even sadder the second time around. The poor old lady's heart was breaking.

Dad made sympathetic sounds. "It's shameful, isn't it?" he said in his important-business voice. "A poor old woman without a dog and just look at them across the way. Leave their dog and run off for a week. Some people don't appreciate what they have."

"They asked me to mind him," Martha said.

"It's still a shame," Dad insisted. "I don't know why we had to get stuck with crazy people like that as neighbors."

"Dad," Martha asked suddenly, "why do you keep calling the Roses crazy? You never explained."

Dad looked as if he didn't want to explain. He looked at Mom and then back at Martha. "Well, they have a bad reputation. They've bought a couple of houses around town and then complained that they were cheated by the sellers."

Martha thought about this. "But maybe they were," she said. "Remember when you and Mom were looking at houses? You said how some people hid things that were wrong with their houses, so they could make them sell. Remember the time you discovered the big hole in the roof that had been covered over with fake brick?"

"It wasn't anything like that, Marth," Dad said.

"Then what was it?"

Dad paused. "Ghosts," he said at last. Martha could feel her mouth drop open and she hastily closed it before Dad could notice. "They said the houses were haunted. It's ridiculous. They resold the houses and the new owners have never complained. The Roses are troublemakers."

"But I don't suppose it's right to call them crazy," Mom said. "It's not nice to put labels on people. They can't help the way they are. And they have been fair to Martha."

Dad was not convinced. "Time will tell," he said. "Don't be surprised if they start the same ghost game all over again here."

Mom laughed. She looked out the kitchen window at the Rose house. "How silly. Can you imagine anything sillier than thinking a house like that is haunted?"

Dad joined her laughing.

Martha didn't know whether to laugh or cry.

12.

Dilemma.

She looked up the word in the dictionary. She remembered it from once when Jemima said she was in a dilemma about which blue jeans to wear to a party.

A dilemma was when you had to make a choice between things and none of the things was any good. It sure was a good way to describe the blue-jean problem. And it fit Martha's problem now. She didn't like any of the choices she had.

After dinner she'd asked Mom to see the picture of the old lady's dog and even though it was a sort of blurry photograph, it looked an awful lot like Buster. The lady's dog was called an Australian shepherd, which was a sheepdog that wasn't like a St. Bernard. And his name wasn't Buster either. It was Rocky.

Looking at the picture gave her a burst of courage and she insisted in a loud voice that it was Jemima's turn to do the dishes. Everyone was so startled by it, they didn't argue. She left Jemima grumbling quietly at the sink and went upstairs and locked herself in her room. She made a list of choices.

1. Tell Mom and Dad about the ghost.
2. Don't tell them and let them think the Roses are crazy.
3. Tell Teddy that Buster belongs to a poor old lady.
4. Don't tell him and let the poor old lady die of a broken heart.

She read the list over and over, but none of it was any good. Only bad. If she told about the ghost, Mom and Dad would think *she* was crazy. Or they'd get mad at her for going into a dangerous place like a haunted house without telling them. If she told Teddy, he'd throw the biggest windbag fit ever.

On the other hand, how could Mom be absolutely sure the old lady was so nice? Maybe she only put on an act to fool Mom so she could get Buster back. She could be like the witch in Hansel and Gretel, who gave the kids candy and acted nice when she was really horrible. Maybe poor Buster had to run away, like Teddy thought.

The only thing to do was check it out.

Martha got a new piece of paper and wrote down a plan.

1. Secretly call Buster by the name Rocky and see if he comes.
2. Tell Teddy that maybe Buster belongs to this old lady on Pineapple Street. (She underlined *maybe* three times.)
3. Take Teddy and visit the old lady to see if she's really a witch.

4. Keep the photograph of Buster a secret until absolutely necessary.

Martha felt better. Now she had some things she could do. And since she was making plans, she'd better figure out what to do tomorrow night. Even if the ghost had really disappeared, they could still give Denise and The Blot a scare. All it took was a little imagination.

Jemima yelled upstairs that there was a phone call for her. She told Martha to hurry the heck up because Mellow was going to call.

Martha pulled the telephone into the closet under the stairs so she could talk privately, just the way Jemima always did. She cleared a space among the snow boots and rubber galoshes and sat down. The hems of the family's winter coats and woolen scarves tickled her head.

She explained to Teddy that they could make ghostly noises and scare Denise and Phyllis, even if the ghost was gone.

At first Teddy wasn't too enthusiastic. But when he began thinking about hiding upstairs and making hideous moans and rattling chains, he got happier.

So, for the third time that night, Martha had to write down a plan.

1. Teddy hides upstairs in the Rose house.
2. Martha tells The Blot they have to feed the neighbor's dog.
3. Jemima suggests she and Denise come along for the fun of it.

4. Teddy makes horrible sounds and throws chains around.
5. When Denise and The Blot are really scared, everyone runs away.
6. Teddy sneaks out and goes home, not forgetting to lock door. Leave key under mat.

She read the plan back to Teddy.

"Sounds okay. Except for one thing."

"What?"

"I think you should warn them a little." When Martha began to protest, he added, "Not a lot, but to get them in the mood, you know? You and Jemima could tell them about some legend or something."

"You mean like the ghost in 'The Legend of Sleepy Hollow'?"

"That's the idea."

"How about the Moaner of Melody Woods?" Martha suggested.

"Or the Upstairs Groaner."

"The Bedroom Banshee."

"The Ghost Who Gargled Near Green Road," Teddy said, really getting into it.

The closet door shook and Martha jumped. "Pssssst," Jemima said.

Martha opened the door a crack. "We're busy. We're discussing the plan."

"Listen," Jemima said. "That dog is howling out there. You'd better do something about it. It's giving me the creeps."

Martha had a terrible thought. If Mom went outside

and looked at Buster, she might start thinking how much he looked like the old lady's dog, Rocky.

"Gotta go," she said to Ted. "We'll talk more in school."

"I hope this isn't going to be too authentic," Jemima said, hanging up the phone and picking it up again to make sure there was a dial tone so Mellow could get through. "I mean, I want to scare Denise, not myself."

"There's nothing to be scared of," Martha said. "It's all in the mind."

Jemima looked doubtful but the phone rang and it was Mellow, so she disappeared into the closet.

Martha got a flashlight and went outside. The porch light cast a nice orange glow all over the yard, but across the way the Roses' yard was in darkness.

She wasn't going to act silly like Jemima. She marched over, planning to call out, "Rocky," as a test. But almost immediately Buster came running over, jumping up and giving slobbery kisses.

"Come on, boy, time for bed."

It was a little creepy inside the house. She and Teddy should have left a light on. But Buster didn't seem to mind. He went right over to his water dish and started slurping up big gulps.

Now might be a good time, while he was busy drinking. She crept into the hall outside the kitchen door and called, "Rocky?"

Buster came running, tail wagging.

Martha felt a pang of disappointment. "Well," she said, "maybe you really are you."

Buster sneezed and went back to his water dish.

Martha went down the hall to the arched opening to the living room. She felt the air stir.

Could it be here?

The harp strings pinged. The living room looked very black.

She didn't care if she was acting like Jemima or not. She shouted, "Buster!"

He came running. He gave a bark and the harp strings stopped.

"Thanks, boy," Martha said, hugging him.

Then she realized that it didn't really matter what she called the dog. Buster, Rocky, boy . . . maybe he'd answer to anything. So there was no telling if he was *the* dog or just *a* dog.

After the caper tomorrow night she and Teddy would have to go to see the old lady and find out for sure.

13.

Martha's dad's favorite expression was "Planning counts." Whenever there was a disaster, like the time Jemima gave a disco party and ten girls and only one boy showed up, or when they drove to the beach without their bathing suits, Dad said it wouldn't have happened if they'd planned better.

Dad was right, Martha thought. On Tuesday afternoon everything went wrong.

First of all Mom was working at home in the kitchen after school instead of at the newspaper office. She wanted to be there because of Phyllis, she said. Which was okay at first because with Mom around, Martha didn't have to constantly think up things to say to The Blot. Mom did a lot of the talking. "Would you like more cookies, Phyllis?" "How about more milk?" "Isn't Melody Woods a nice place?"

The Blot crammed at least three dozen of Mom's homemade oatmeal cookies into her vampire mouth. She drank two huge glasses of milk and didn't even bother to wipe off the milk mustache.

Mom didn't ask Martha to clear the table. She took the plates and glasses to the sink herself. And happened to look out the window.

"Why, there's Ted," she exclaimed, "going into the Roses'."

Of course, that instantly caused a disaster. Martha had to say Ted had volunteered to feed Buster. So what was she going to use as an excuse later on?

Then Jemima came home and made strange eyebrow motions until Martha finally caught on that she wanted to talk privately. They met in the downstairs powder room.

"Denise couldn't come!" Jemima screeched in a whisper. "Now what am I gonna do?"

"I'll think of something," Martha said, but she doubted it. The Blot was already banging on the door.

"I just know she sneaked off with Mellow," Jemima wailed.

"You can't be sure."

The Blot banged the door again. "What are you two doing in there?"

"For crumb's sake," Jemima cried, and flung the door open. "We're having a tragedy in here, that's all!"

The Blot's eyes bugged out. Jemima stomped off.

Martha suggested they go upstairs to play some games.

"I don't like games," said the Blot.

She refused to play, even though Martha took every single game down from her closet shelf and spread them out. Disaster number three.

Martha sat on her bed and watched Phyllis snoop around the bedroom, picking things up and putting them down in the wrong places.

Finally, she couldn't stand it anymore. The heck with ghosts and plans to scare people. She needed Teddy's help or she would never survive the evening.

"Let's go next door," she said to Phyllis.

"What for?"

"I have to take care of the neighbor's dog."

"I thought your friend the weirdo was doing it."

"It's . . . er . . . really my job."

"Oh, I know," Phyllis said, nodding her head. "You have to check up on him, right? A weirdo could only do a weirdo job." She thought this was really funny and almost got hysterical laughing. Martha observed that she looked exactly like Miss Hatton, the teacher they hated most.

As they walked across the driveway, Martha was surprised to hear Phyllis say, "What a spooky-looking place." But it didn't matter anymore. She just wanted Teddy to help her out of five hours of Blot-boredom. She pounded on the door, because she'd given Ted the key.

The door swung open by itself. It even made an eerie squeak. Well, at least Ted had been doing his job.

"Teddy?" Martha called out. There was no answer. But then, there wouldn't be. He was upstairs hiding and probably wondering why Martha was ruining everything by calling out his name.

Phyllis was looking around, up at the big ugly hall mirror and at the ceilings with their plaster flower decorations. Martha had an urge to give a Teddy-lecture and start telling her about Lincrusta and balustrades. She giggled. Immediately there was a moan from upstairs. It sounded so phony, she couldn't help but giggle again.

"What was that?" The Blot asked.

"I didn't hear anything," Martha said.

"So where's this dog you're supposed to be taking care of?" Phyllis asked.

73

Martha realized that Buster hadn't come running. He wasn't locked in the kitchen, either, because she could see the door partly open. Probably Teddy had taken him upstairs. Which was dopey because the excuse was supposed to have been feeding the dog. Oh, well, it didn't matter now.

"He's around," Martha said. "Hey, Ted!" she yelled up the staircase. "You can come down, it's all off!"

"What's off?" Phyllis asked suspiciously.

Then came another moan. This one was better than the first, and louder. It even sent a shiver up Martha's spine. She felt The Blot's cold dry hand clutching her arm.

"You must have heard that," Phyllis said.

"I guess so."

Phyllis looked at her. "Aren't you scared?"

"You're not afraid of ghosts, are you?"

Phyllis nodded her head. She looked pretty nervous. And when the next howl came from above, accompanied by the crashing of chains, Phyllis turned green. "Of course I'm afraid of ghosts," she said. "I'm not stupid."

That made Martha mad. "I'm not stupid either."

They started an argument about who was calling who stupid but such a terrible howling, growling, yowling, and bawling was coming from upstairs that they couldn't hear each other talk.

"Teddy, for Pete's sake, shut up!" Martha yelled at the top of her lungs.

The Blot's green face turned bright red. "Teddy?" she yelped. "You rats. You were just trying to scare me."

And then, to Martha's astonishment, she burst into tears.

74

"Gosh," Martha said. "Gosh. I'm sorry."

Phyllis sat down on the bottom step, snuffling and shaking. The noise upstairs continued.

"He's really overdoing it," Martha said, and she began to stomp upstairs to tell him to knock it off once and for all.

At that moment Teddy appeared. But not from upstairs where he should have been. From the kitchen, downstairs. His cheeks were red with cold air and he was carrying two thin rusty chains. Buster was beside him.

"What's all the racket?" he asked, eyes wide with wonder.

"Oh, my," Martha said. And she sat down on the step just above Phyllis. Her heart began to beat very fast.

Suddenly, the noise stopped.

The three of them looked at each other in the silence, almost afraid to move in case the noise started again.

"You mean, it wasn't you?" Martha whispered.

Teddy shook his head. "I was out in the shed, looking for props."

Phyllis sniffed and wiped her nose on the back of her hand.

"Then who was it?" Martha asked.

"The ghost, of course," Phyllis said. "Boy, you two are really stupid."

"It was like the ghost knew our plans all along," Teddy said, a little later after they locked up the Rose house and went to sit in Martha's yard. Buster ran around, sniffing trees.

"It sure made more noise than it did before," said Martha.

"Why'd you want to scare me?" Phyllis asked.

Martha and Teddy looked at each other. They had to confess.

"Just for a joke," said Martha. "I guess it wasn't very funny."

Teddy gave her a stare as if to remind her what he'd said about making people feel bad.

"Some joke," said Phyllis. Then she smiled a little, showing her vampire teeth. "Of course, it was fun."

"It was?" Teddy asked.

"Sure. Listen, we could get some kids over and *really* have fun."

"You mean, scare them?"

"Yeah."

Teddy rolled his eyes. "But it's a dirty trick," he said. "I mean, someone could get really scared."

"That's the idea," said Phyllis. "Only, they wouldn't really mind." She began listing all the kids they could scare and telling how they could have big Halloween parties. Finally, Martha broke in.

"There's only one problem," she said, when Phyllis finally stopped talking. "We have eight days to get rid of the ghost."

"Or else the problem is going to be bigger than big," said Teddy.

Once you started telling the truth, it seemed like you couldn't stop, thought Martha. Here they were explaining the whole thing to The Blot, of all people, telling her how Teddy had fooled Mrs. Rose into believing the stray dog was a ghostbuster, just to get him a home for ten days.

Well, Phyllis wasn't all that bad, Martha also thought. She was a good sport at least.

Phyllis listened and when they finished talking she didn't say anything for a moment.

"Pretty hard to believe, huh?" said Ted.

"Nope," said Phyllis.

"But as you can see, there's no solution. It's obvious this ghost knows all. It probably knows what we're saying right now. There's no way we can get it to leave before the Roses come back." Teddy poked at the ground with a stick and Buster came and grabbed it and ran off.

Phyllis looked them over with her beady brown eyes. Like we're two cantaloupes, Martha thought. She was afraid the Blot might give them a pinch to see if they were ripe enough.

"I know what you should do," Phyllis announced.

"What?" Martha said.

"What?" Teddy asked.

"Go to see Mrs. Wish."

Teddy and Martha sighed. "So who's that?" they asked.

"This old lady who knows all about ghosts and telling fortunes," Phyllis said. "She lives way over on Pineapple Street."

"An old lady on Pineapple Street?" Martha asked. "Does she have a dog?"

"I never saw her myself," Phyllis replied. "But my mom goes to have her fortune told and the last time she went, she was mad 'cause her coat got full of dog hair."

Teddy piped up. "Who cares if she has a dog or not? We don't need any advice from old ladies."

So Martha had to tell him about her mom's interview and the picture of the dog named Rocky. "It's only a maybe that it's Buster," she said, emphasizing the word *maybe*.

"It sounds fishy to me. Mrs. Wish sounds even fishier. It sounds a lot like Mrs. Witch."

"We'll have to check, Ted," Martha said gently. "Anyway, it will be in the newspaper tomorrow, with the picture."

Buster came back with the stick in his mouth and Teddy grabbed him and hugged him. "I don't think we should visit a witch. She'll put a spell on us."

"My mother goes there all the time," Phyllis said, "and she never came back with a spell on her. Only dog hair."

"We'll go over tomorrow after school," Martha said, "and get it settled once and for all."

"I'll come too," said Phyllis.

Teddy had to agree, although halfheartedly. Martha realized he probably hadn't put up the ads on telephone poles the way he was supposed to. He really had a thing about Buster. Or Rocky. Whatever his name was.

14.

It turned out The Blot wasn't half bad. She acted fairly okay at dinner and laughed at Dad's jokes. She didn't eat too much and she didn't make comments about Jemima. Jemima sat through dinner with her head practically in her plate and didn't even bother to do *he loves me, he loves me not* with her Brussels sprouts.

Phyllis actually ate the Brussels sprouts as if she liked them. Which wasn't normal. It was also not normal to offer to help with the dishes, which is what Phyllis did when dinner was over. Jemima ran up to her room, as usual.

Mom said no, guests didn't have to help and that she and Martha could be excused. "Do your homework and then play some games," Mom suggested.

"Don't you have a TV?" Phyllis asked Martha as they went upstairs.

"Yes, but we don't watch it on weeknights unless there's something special on."

"Bad reception, huh? We have cable."

"Mom says it's not worth watching most of the time. She says it doesn't do anything to stimulate our brains."

Phyllis nodded her head as if she suddenly understood. "I guess that's why you're so hot on games."

"I don't play games that much," Martha said as they

walked into her bedroom. She noticed Phyllis looked puzzled at all the board games spread out on the floor and bed. Martha hurriedly stacked them up.

"We could play one if you want to," Phyllis said. "Maybe we should ask your sister too. She looked real sad at dinner. Did she fail a test or something?"

Martha laughed. The Blot was really weird. Probably weirder than Teddy, the original Weirdo. Probably everyone was weird when you got to know them.

"I don't think Jemima is in the mood for games," she said. "She's having problems with her boyfriend."

"You mean that guy Mellow Rollings?"

Martha looked up from the games she was stacking. "How'd you know?"

"I see them in the mall a lot. My mom works there on Saturdays and she brings me along. I didn't know she was your sister until I saw her tonight. So what's the problem?"

The Blot might not be half bad, but Martha wasn't sure she wanted to discuss family business with her. "I don't know," she said, and climbed up on a chair to stick the games back on the closet shelf.

"She's going to be really surprised," Phyllis said.

"Who is?"

"Your sister. I shouldn't really tell."

"Tell what?"

Phyllis shook her head. "Nope, I can't tell."

"It's just about the worst thing," Martha said, "to start telling something and then say you can't."

"Well . . ." Phyllis considered. "Okay. I'll tell if you promise not to tell Jemima." She gave Martha a lopsided grin that made her look like Miss Hatton again. Martha changed her mind about wanting to hear anything The Blot had to say.

"Forget it. I know what it is, anyway."

"No, you don't."

"Yes, I do."

"You absolutely don't!" Phyllis said, getting mad.

Martha climbed down off the chair and slammed the closet door shut. "It's about Denise and Mellow. Denise is trying to steal him from my sister, right? See, I do too know."

"That's absolutely wrong," Phyllis said. "But you can think it if you want to." She started humming and looking at her nails. She picked out one that wasn't short enough and bit it.

"It's true," Martha said.

Phyllis hummed. "It's okay with me."

Martha felt like growling, just the way the ghost had done earlier. "Okay, okay, I give up. What's the story?"

Phyllis glanced at the door. Then she beckoned Martha closer.

"It's this," she whispered with Brussels-sprout breath. "They're planning a surprise party for your sister's birthday. They bought all the invitations and balloons and stuff at the store where my mother works. They got black and silver decorations. They're your sister's favorite colors, I heard Mellow say."

"Really and truly?"

"Cross my heart," Phyllis said, and gave her a big vampire grin.

"Now what should I do?"

Phyllis shrugged. "Nothing. You're not supposed to tell about surprise parties. It ruins the surprise."

"I know that," Martha said impatiently. "But it's a shame to see Jemima so sad. It's another week and half until her birthday."

"Don't tell her," The Blot said heartlessly. "It will make it even better when the day comes."

Martha wasn't sure. It seemed coldhearted. But it sure would be a big surprise when Jemima found out that Mellow loved her after all. Unless one thing. "Suppose Jemima decides to get a new boyfriend before the party?"

Phyllis shook her head. "You can't get a boyfriend that fast," she said. "It takes time and there are a lot of uncertainties."

"How come you know so much about it?"

"I watch TV," Phyllis said.

They had cocoa and Mom's special healthful granola bars before bed. Jemima came down to the kitchen for a pig-out. She said she was giving up her diet because it didn't matter anymore. What difference did it make if she was as fat as an elephant, anyway?

"Uh . . . but . . . er . . . Jemima," Martha started to say, but Phyllis gave her a kick under the table.

"You never know," Phyllis said through a mouthful of granola bar. "Prince Charming could be just around the corner."

Jemima looked at her. "For crumb's sake," she said, and stomped out.

"Poor Jemima," Martha said.

"You can't get fat as an elephant in a week and a half," Phyllis said. "It takes even longer than it does to get a boyfriend."

Martha felt exhausted. It had been a tough day, as Dad

would say, what with the three disasters and the ghost and The Blot suddenly turning out the way she had. Martha was ready when Mom said it was time for bed. She didn't even have the strength to be disgusted when The Blot spit toothpaste all over the bathroom sink.

Martha climbed into her bed and Phyllis got into the folding cot they always kept for guests.

"All comfy?" Mom asked. She gave them each a kiss good-night. Martha thought yeeccch, but then mothers probably didn't notice things like vampire teeth and Brussels-sprout breath.

Martha was almost asleep when she remembered the question that had been bugging her ever since Mrs. Blott had phoned to ask if Phyllis could spend the night. She'd wanted to ask it before but no time had seemed right. Now, in the dark, it seemed easier.

"Phyllis?" she whispered. "Are you awake?"

"Yes."

"Could I ask you a question? Why didn't you spend the night at Jenny's instead of here? She's your best friend."

There was a silence and Martha thought maybe The Blot had fallen asleep. Then, at last, her voice came through the dark room, sounding a little breathless.

"Because she only likes me for my house and pool and cats. She'd never want to be friends with me if I lived in Grape Hill Apartments near her."

Martha was astonished. That's just what she had thought when she found out Jenny wanted to be best friends with Phyllis, last year. She'd even told Mom but Mom had just laughed.

"So I asked my mother to call you," Phyllis went on. "Because you already have a house."

"A cat too," Martha said. "Only, she's never home."

"I know your cat," Phyllis said. "She comes to my house a lot. I once took a splinter out of her paw. I gave her some milk. Was that okay?"

"Of course it's okay," Martha said. "Thanks for doing it."

There was a long silence and then Phyllis said, "I know nobody really likes me." Her voice sounded a little funny and Martha hoped she wasn't going to cry.

"Don't be silly," she said, to cover up.

"It's true," Phyllis said. "And I know why. It's because of my vampire teeth."

Martha gasped.

"Isn't it?"

"You're really weird, Phyllis," she said, because she didn't trust herself to say something else. "I mean, you're weirder than Teddy ever was." Then she felt bad so she added, "But weird people are very interesting."

"I'm glad you think so," said Phyllis.

"Good night," Martha said.

Phyllis didn't answer. Then, when Martha felt herself drifting off into a dream, she heard her voice again.

"Do you think," Phyllis was saying, "we could be friends? I could go to the dentist and ask him to saw off the ends of my teeth."

For a moment Martha said nothing. And then she laughed. Phyllis started to laugh too. Finally, they couldn't control it anymore. They had to put tissues in their mouths to stop from waking the whole house up.

15.

It felt strange to be walking to school with Phyllis. She told Martha that her father usually drove her on his way to work. "But walking is nicer," she added.

"My mom says it's healthier," Martha said. "My mom's a health nut, in case you didn't notice."

"My mom's nutty too," Phyllis confided. "Like getting her fortune told. She's hoping to win the lottery so we can all move to Florida."

They were telling each other things, secrets about their families. It was the kind of thing friends do. Martha realized she wouldn't be able to call Phyllis The Blot anymore. You couldn't call your friend a name like that. It was like Mom said. You shouldn't put labels on people. When you thought of The Blot, you thought yeeccch. When you thought Phyllis, it seemed okay.

Teddy was waiting on the corner at Ducktrap Road. He looked glum. He didn't like the idea of having to visit Pineapple Street that afternoon. He tried to make excuses.

"Maybe I'll have a lot of homework," he said. "Mrs. Ellery might give me extra math."

"Why should she?" Phyllis said. "You always get the

best grades in math. I'm the one who should get extra work."

"It's about time you admitted it," Teddy said huffily. "I saw you cheating on the last test."

They stopped and glared at each other and Martha's heart sank. It looked like Phyllis might turn out to be her friend. But it would be awful if Teddy didn't get along with her. What would she do if her two best friends hated each other?

"Anyway, it didn't count," Phyllis said. "The person I copied from failed the test."

Teddy's eyes goggled behind his glasses as he tried to think up something to say.

"Come on, guys," Martha urged. "We'll be late for school."

The day seemed like forever. And it was really weird. Instead of sitting with Jenny at lunchtime, Phyllis came over to Martha and Teddy's table. She unwrapped the lunch Martha's mom had packed for her and inspected it.

"Told you my mom was a health nut," Martha said, afraid Phyllis was going to criticize. "You don't have to eat it. You won't hurt my feelings."

"It looks delicious," Phyllis said, and immediately began chomping on the raw carrots with her vampire teeth. Martha had to remind herself she shouldn't think that way anymore.

"Usually," Phyllis said, spraying carrot juice around, "I have to make my own lunch. It's boring to eat what you make yourself."

Right away, Teddy disagreed. "I always make my own lunch," he said. "And I make my own dinner too. My dinners are never boring."

"Are you two gonna have another fight?" Martha asked.

Teddy looked surprised. "We're having a discussion, like we had yesterday in reading group. Mrs. Ellery said we're all entitled to our own opinions, remember?"

"I don't think she said exactly that. But go ahead and have your discussion. Just don't give me indigestion."

"I'd never think of raw carrots for lunch," Phyllis said. "I don't think my mother ever bought a carrot."

"How could a person never buy a carrot?" asked Teddy.

"My mother only buys things for the microwave," Phyllis replied. "We don't have raw things at our house."

Teddy frowned. Martha changed the subject before he could give a lecture on vegetables. She asked Ted if he'd looked at the town map as he'd promised, to find out how to get to Pineapple Street.

"I did," Ted reported. "And it's really far. We might have to take a bus."

"Walking's healthier," Phyllis said, now chewing on the celery sticks. "Martha's mom said so."

"Walking is fine," Teddy said, "but not all the way to Pineapple Street. We'll never get home in time for dinner. I'm trying a new meatball recipe. It takes time to smush the meat up with the ketchup and eggs. And then you have to roll the meat into these little balls. And then you have to fry the balls until golden brown—"

"The microwave is a lot simpler," said Phyllis.

"I don't know if I have enough money for a bus," Martha said.

"It costs eighty-five cents each way," Teddy said. "I called the bus company to check. I got the number of the

87

bus too." He pulled a crumpled piece of paper out of his pocket and smoothed it out on the lunch table. "I only had two bucks in my piggy bank."

Phyllis gave a little screech. "You have a piggy bank?"

"So what? It's a genuine antique piggy bank, if you want to know!"

Here they go again, thought Martha. She searched her pockets and came up with a quarter and two dimes.

"We'll have to go back to my house first," she said.

Teddy shook his head. "The bus runs on schedule from Bailey Avenue. If we don't make the three-fifteen, we'll have to wait until four o'clock."

"Rats," said Martha. "I wish you'd told me. Why didn't you phone me so I could bring enough money?" She was annoyed.

"I did!" Teddy shouted at her. "Your line was busy last night and busy this morning. I figured it was off the hook."

"Well, it wasn't my fault," Martha yelled back. "You know Jemima hogs the phone."

"Now look who's fighting," Phyllis said in a cheerful voice. "Listen, there's nothing to worry about. I have all the cash we need." And she flipped open a wallet and showed them a whole bunch of crisp green bills.

Teddy gawked at them. Phyllis gave a real vampire grin. Martha tried not to think bad things, but she could see that Phyllis was trying to act like a big deal. In fact, maybe Phyllis was also trying to steal Teddy away from her.

Then Teddy put on his supercilious look, which he did better than anyone Martha knew.

"The bus only takes exact change," he said.

Hooray, Teddy, Martha inwardly cheered.

"That's okay," said Phyllis. "We'll stop at the Sweet Shop first. You two can have anything you want . . . sodas, candy, even a banana split. I'll treat because I'm rich."

"Oh, brother," said Martha. It was a lucky thing the bell rang. Teddy thought so too. He gave Martha an eyebrow look and hurried to dump his trash in the basket.

Martha stood up to empty her tray but Phyllis lagged behind. It wasn't nice to leave a new friend in the lurch, she supposed. "Come on, Phyllis, let's get going."

Phyllis picked up her scrunched-up foil and brown paper bag. When she turned around, her eyes looked all shiny, as if big tears might come spilling out of them.

"It was really nice of you to offer to treat," Martha said, feeling bad. "I think I'll order a chocolate shake."

"I thought it would be fun," Phyllis said in a weepy voice.

"It will be. And it's a good idea. We'll need extra strength to go see this Mrs. Wish."

Phyllis perked up a little. Martha wondered if someday she was going to have to explain to her that maybe it wasn't just vampire teeth that kept her from having friends. Another thing Dad always said. Nobody likes someone who acts like a big deal.

16.

The bus rattled and Martha bounced around on her seat. It didn't feel so good, after a double chocolate shake.

When they'd got on the bus, Martha had felt like a million butterflies were fighting in her stomach and she was all mixed up about what she expected to happen with Mrs. Wish. It would be nice if she turned out to really be a poor old lady. They'd make her happy by returning her dog. Then again, that would make Teddy sad. But if Mrs. Wish turned out to be a nasty old witch, they could all be in danger of having a spell put on them.

By the time they got to the corner of Pineapple Street, all Martha could think of was getting off. She wanted fresh air and a walk to make the chocolate shake in her stomach stop shaking.

"Here's your stop, kids," the bus driver called out.

They got off and looked around. Everything looked old-fashioned. Little houses on a little winding street. White fences and funny lampposts. Big old trees leaning way over the fences and making puddles of darkness underneath. It was all a little scary.

"Is this place for real?" said Teddy.

"Yeah," Phyllis agreed. "It looks like the pictures in a fairy-tale book."

"Well, let's hope it's not Hansel and Gretel," Martha said.

Martha had a feeling they all would have liked to hold hands. But that would be too silly. So they just walked along the narrow winding street, looking for number 13.

At first they were kind of talking and laughing, making jokes about how they should leave a trail of bread crumbs. But after a while nobody wanted to talk. The sun was going down and the trees looked even taller and fatter and the darkness underneath them got blacker.

"It's not a fairy tale, it's a horror movie," Teddy said. "I mean, look at the facts. This old lady lives on the spookiest street in town, she tells fortunes, and the number of her house is thirteen." He stopped in his tracks. "I think we should go back. It's going to take me a long time to make the meatballs."

Martha stopped too. She had just spied Mrs. Wish's house at the end of the street. It looked exactly like the gingerbread house in Hansel and Gretel.

Phyllis made a horse-snort sound in her nose. "You guys!" she hooted. "Did you forget about my mother? So far she hasn't been turned into a gingerbread cookie."

"Witches are always cautious with adults," Teddy said. "It's poor innocent children like us they want."

"Come on." Martha sighed. "Let's get it over with."

Silently, they marched up to number 13, opened the gate in the white picket fence, walked up the path, and rapped on the door.

There was no answer.

"Good," Teddy said. "That's that, let's go."

"She's old," Martha reminded him. "It probably takes her a long time to get to the door."

"I hear something," Phyllis said.

The door opened slowly. First the tip of a nose poked out. Martha, Teddy, and Phyllis took a step backward. A sharp pointy chin appeared, then two very dark but wary eyes. A bony hand reached around the doorjamb. It had long red nails and a lot of diamond rings. Martha, Teddy, and Phyllis stepped back again, and Teddy tripped.

The bony hand reached out farther to grab him. A whole slew of bangle bracelets clanked together.

"I've gotta go," Teddy said in a squeaky voice. "My meatballs are waiting."

"Meatballs?" a quavery voice asked, and the door was flung open wide. Standing there was the old lady. Except for the blood-red nails and jewelry, she looked like some-body's kind old grandmother. Her white hair was wispy and pulled back into a grandmotherly bun. Her dress was sort of colonial looking, with a high neck and long sleeves. It was made of a nice safe grandmotherly-type printed cotton. The lady was leaning on a cane. From behind her came delicious smells of cinnamon and spice.

Martha got her wits back first. "Hi," she said. "We came to inquire about your lost dog."

The lady smiled. It cleared all scary ideas of witches out of Martha's mind. But she reminded herself to be careful. You couldn't tell a book by its cover, after all.

Mrs. Wish invited them in. The front room of the house was cozy, with big stuffed armchairs and lots of little colorful rugs. There were pictures all over, on the fireplace, the tables, and along the windowsills, stuck in between pots of dusty-looking plants and dried up cactus. All the pictures were of dogs. Martha peered closer, hoping they would not all be of Buster. A million pictures of Buster would give Teddy a shock.

"My babies," Mrs. Wish exclaimed when she saw Martha squinting at the photographs. Teddy jumped a little and looked around suspiciously. Mrs. Wish told them all to sit down, and she would bring them some apple cider and freshly baked cookies. Teddy rolled his eyes and tried to signal Martha. He mouthed something at her but she couldn't understand.

"Poison," he whispered hoarsely as soon as Mrs. Wish was out of the room. She came right back in again, and Teddy's cheeks grew red.

"Here he is," she said, sticking one of the framed pictures into Teddy's hands. "Peruse that while I get the refreshments."

Teddy glared at the photograph. "It doesn't look at all like him."

Phyllis craned her neck to get a look. "Nope, he's right," she agreed.

But when Martha looked she could see it was Buster. He was younger in the picture, more puppyish. But there was his tongue lolling out the side of his mouth and the same intelligent eyes that seemed to understand everything you said. "Well," she said to Teddy, wanting to break the news gently.

They heard Mrs. Wish clanking dishes in the kitchen.

"Should we eat the stuff?" Ted asked.

Martha looked around the cozy room. She realized it was all perfectly safe. Her mom and Phyllis's mom had been here. They were just letting themselves get carried away. "Of course," she said, and added, "I think we'd better be honest, Ted. We're going to have to let Mrs. Wish take a look at Buster for herself."

"She might try to fool us," Teddy said.

"Buster will know if he belongs to her," Phyllis offered.

Teddy shook his head. "You can't rely on *him*! He'd go along with anybody, just like he came along with me. He can't be trusted!"

Mrs. Wish came back and asked if they could come into the kitchen to help with the tray. "I can't carry it, you see," she said, holding up her cane.

They trooped into the kitchen. It was just the way Martha's mom had described it, very old-fashioned. A lot like the kitchen in the Rose house. No sparkly counters and no microwave, no refrigerator with an automatic ice-water dispenser in the door. Phyllis looked around and bared her teeth in a disapproving vampire smirk.

"Wow," Teddy said. He went over to a huge stove that took up almost an entire wall. It had eight burners, a griddle, and three ovens. It was like a battleship. "Wow," Teddy said again. "I bet you could run a restaurant on this stove."

"It was in a restaurant once," Mrs. Wish said. "Are you interested in cooking?"

"As a matter of fact, I am," Teddy replied, and began telling Mrs. Wish about his chocolate-cake disasters.

"Would you like to see the oven?" Mrs. Wish asked. "You could bake a lot of good cakes in here." She reached down and opened the oven door. It was a very big oven. She put her hand on Teddy's shoulders as he bent down to have a look inside.

Martha gave a little yelp. She couldn't help it. It looked a lot like the witch trying to push Hansel into the oven. Teddy must have realized it, too, because he straightened up real quick and stopped talking. Mrs. Wish looked puzzled. "Let's have our treats in the living room," she said.

Teddy and Martha exchanged looks. Teddy took the tray. "Thanks for saving me," he whispered. "That was a close call."

"It was nothing," Martha whispered back. "I just got carried away."

Mrs. Wish invited them to sit down again and enjoy their cider and cookies. "I love baking cookies," Mrs. Wish told them. "I make a batch every week. I hope you like these. They're fudge chip."

"Do you ever make gingerbread boys?" Teddy asked, and Martha kicked him. Phyllis was busy stuffing her face with cookies and croaked out a laugh. "You guys," she said, spitting crumbs all over Mrs. Wish's pretty rugs.

"Now tell me," Mrs. Wish said. "Have you found my Rocky?"

Teddy immediately lost his appetite, even though he thought the fudge chip cookies were delicious. He pretended he didn't understand. "I don't know any Rocky. Do you?" he asked Martha.

"Rocky's the name of Mrs. Wish's dog," Martha explained. Then she told Mrs. Wish who she was.

"Betsy Lewis's little girl!" Mrs. Wish exclaimed. "Oh, dear, I've forgotten my manners. We've never introduced ourselves, have we?"

They had to tell Mrs. Wish their names and she insisted on getting up to shake hands with them all. She told them her name hadn't always been Mrs. Wish. Once it has been a very long name with a lot of *Z* 's and *W* 's in it.

"Nobody could pronounce it, so I shortened it to Wish," she explained. "It sounded like good luck to me. Everybody likes a wish."

"Yeah, but they don't always come true," Teddy said.

Mrs. Wish leaned toward him and her bangle bracelets clanked. "That sounds sad. Tell me what you wished for, Ted."

"That Buster wouldn't be your dog." He looked around at them defiantly. It was better to say it out loud.

"Is Buster the dog you found?" Mrs. Wish asked.

Teddy nodded. "He might be your dog and he might not be. You'd have to sort of prove it." He gulped. "If you wouldn't mind."

Mrs. Wish shook her head. "Of course I wouldn't mind. It's a very sensible request." She put her hand with its long red fingernails up to her cheek. "Let's see. He's black and white and very smart. And he has no tail."

"I thought all dogs were born with tails," Phyllis said, helping herself to the cookies left on Teddy's plate.

"Rocky's tail was removed," said Mrs. Wish. "That's what they do for the Australian shepherd breed."

"Removed?" Teddy repeated.

"Yes, cut off, so when the dogs herd sheep their tails don't get caught in the burr and bush."

"Cut off?" Teddy asked.

Mrs. Wish looked at him. "Yes. When he was a puppy."

Teddy leapt out of his chair. "That's the most horrible thing I've ever heard."

"Oh, dear," said Mrs. Wish. "I'm sorry I mentioned it. But it didn't hurt him, you know."

Teddy glared at her. "How can you know? It wasn't your tail!"

"There are no sheep around here, anyway," Phyllis piped up, making things worse.

Martha knew she had to do something before everybody had a fit. She leapt out of her chair too. "Excuse him, please, Mrs. Wish. Ted's just awfully worried about Buster. He really likes him and hoped he could keep him."

"It's true," Teddy said, sitting down again. "Buster is black and white and very smart and he has no tail. But you haven't proved everything."

"Is there more?" Mrs. Wish asked.

"More facts," Teddy said. "Like what was he wearing?"

Mrs. Wish thought a moment. "He had his collar on. Blue leather it was."

Martha watched Teddy's face go all crumbly. She felt horrible inside. Mrs. Wish seemed nice enough, but she hadn't been a very good dog owner.

"He wasn't wearing any tags," she said to Mrs. Wish, surprised that her voice sounded so shaky. "A dog should wear tags. If you'd put tags on him, all this wouldn't have happened!" She stopped speaking and gave a big sniff. She had a wish, all right. She wished she didn't feel like crying and that Teddy didn't look like he felt like crying and that Phyllis would stop cramming all those cookies in her big fat mouth!

17.

"You're quite right," Mrs. Wish said. "I told that to myself a hundred times since he's been gone. He has his tags, of course, but I hadn't put them on his new blue collar yet."

Now it looked as if Mrs. Wish was going to cry. The only one who wasn't feeling bad was Phyllis. Although now that all the cookies were gone, she might join in, Martha thought.

It was a surprise that Teddy was the one who recovered first. He took a deep breath and said, "It's best to face facts. Buster sounds like your dog. If he is, you can have him back."

"Thank you, Ted," Mrs. Wish said, patting his hand. "I'm sure you've taken good care of him. But tell me, why did you call him Buster?"

"From ghostbuster," Teddy answered.

Mrs. Wish's eyebrows went up into her wispy white hair.

"It's just something silly," Martha said quickly. It suddenly seemed dopey to be talking about ghosts with Mrs. Wish. She looked too normal, except for the red fingernails. And she had enough trouble with her lost dog and bad leg. It was getting late, anyway. "I think we'd better be going now, or we'll miss the bus."

"But we haven't arranged things yet, about getting Buster—I mean Rocky—back," said Mrs. Wish, looking a little flustered and confused. Martha was glad they weren't going to get her involved with the ghost.

"I'll ask my mom to drive us over," she told the old lady. Mrs. Wish thought this was a good idea.

Then Phyllis butted in. "Maybe you could wait a few days," she said. "Buster's busy doing an important job right now."

"What sort of job?" Mrs. Wish asked.

Martha looked at Ted and he shrugged. "Ghostbusting, if you have to know."

"There's this house," Phyllis went on, "and there's this ghost. It's a real one too. I should know because they tried to scare me to death with it, but anyway your dog is supposed to chase the ghost away before the owners of the house come back." Phyllis beamed at them. "Or else there's gonna be a lot of trouble."

"My word!" Mrs. Wish exclaimed. "A ghost."

"It's nothing," Martha said. "Just a silly idea she got into her head," and she tried to pull Phyllis toward the door.

"That's right," Teddy said, helping to pull. "Whoever heard of anything sillier than a ghost?"

There was a jumble of arms and feet and Phyllis's complaints. They had the door open and were almost out, making a good escape, when they heard Mrs. Wish shout.

"Wait!" she commanded in a very loud voice that didn't sound grandmotherly at all.

Everybody stopped.

"A ghost is not silly," Mrs. Wish said more softly. "A ghost should be taken seriously. A ghost is a ghost."

Martha found herself nodding. She noticed Teddy and Phyllis were nodding too. Phyllis's eyes were bugged out like two fat prunes. Teddy's eyes looked like saucers.

Mrs. Wish seemed to float back into the living room and they all floated in behind her and took their same seats as if they'd been hypnotized. Mrs. Wish put out her hands with their blood-red nails. Her bracelets fell back onto her arms, and for a few moments the echo of their clanking was the only sound in the room.

"Now," she said. "Tell me all."

They told.

At first it felt silly, no matter what Mrs. Wish said. Later, it felt serious. Finally, Martha knew that Mrs. Wish was probably the best ghost psychiatrist they'd ever hope to meet. And probably the only one. And she promised to help.

18.

Mrs. Wish sent them home in a taxi, which she paid for in advance. She promised to come to the Rose house the next afternoon. In the meantime they had to do certain things.

Martha's mom was angry. Martha had to explain how she and Teddy had gone all the way to Pineapple Street to find out if Buster was Mrs. Wish's dog. When Mom heard this, she wasn't any happier.

"Don't tell me those crazy Roses have stolen a poor old lady's dog!"

Martha had to explain some more. She didn't want to tell any lies, but she didn't want to tell the exact truth either. She told Mom how Teddy had found the dog wandering around on Bailey Avenue in danger of getting hit by cars and how Mrs. Rose thought it would be nice to have a watchdog in the house while they were away.

Mom still wasn't happy. "It was nice of you to do all this, Marth, but you should have told me where you were going after school."

"Yes, Mom," Martha agreed. "But we never planned to be so late."

"That's no excuse," Mom said, looking stern. "Mothers get worried, you know."

"I know," Martha said, glad to have a mom who worried. From what she could tell, Teddy's mother didn't worry very much when she left him alone to cook his own dinners, and Phyllis's mom was busy a lot.

"Well. After all this, were you successful?"

"I'm not sure," Martha said.

"If it does turn out to be Mrs. Wish's dog, you'll be famous," Mom said. "I'll write a story about it for the newspaper."

Just when Martha felt like relaxing, she had to get worried again. If Mom did a story, she'd want to interview Mrs. Wish again. And Mrs. Wish would tell all about the ghost in the Rose house and it would all come out how Teddy had fooled Mrs. Rose and how Martha had let him get away with it.

"Ugh," Martha said. "I don't want to be famous."

"That's 'cause you're a crumb-brain," Jemima said, coming into the kitchen. One look at her and you could tell she was in a really bad mood.

"It doesn't hurt to be polite," Mom reprimanded. But Jemima only took a tissue out of her pocket and blew her nose like a train whistle.

"Are you getting a cold?" Mom asked.

"Not really," Jemima said.

Mom rummaged around in her special drawer and came up with a handful of pills. They were the special health vitamins she made everyone take whenever a cold was coming on. "Even if it's an unreally cold, take these," she told Jemima.

To Martha's surprise Jemima swallowed every pill. But maybe it was just as well. Jemima looked a little like a ghost herself. Martha knew it was because she was pining away for Mellow, worried sick that Denise was stealing him. It was hard to resist telling her. Even one little hint would make Jemima happy again.

"What do you think you'll do on your birthday?" Martha asked, trying to be casual.

"I'm baby-sitting," Jemima said.

"On your birthday! For who?"

"Harvey Bender. I said I'd take the job for all day Saturday and stay the night. They're going to some big party in Southport. Ha ha. A big party, get it?" Jemima gave a strange phony laugh and began picking at the salad Mom had put on the table for dinner.

Martha's brain was spinning. This was a terrible development. The surprise party would be spoiled. Someone was going to have to warn Mrs. Bender.

"Stop picking!" Mom scolded.

"I've got to make a phone call," Martha said.

Mrs. Bender's line was busy. Dad came downstairs and opened the hall closet door and said he had to make an important call, so Martha had to come out. Then it was time for dinner. After dinner Jemima planted herself near the phone. It was going to be impossible to phone Mrs. Bender. There would be too many explanations to get through before the message was clear. Jemima was sure to hear.

Martha phoned Phyllis.

"I hope it's not too late to call," Martha said when Phyllis came to the phone. "Was everything okay with your mom when you got home?"

"Sure," Phyllis said. "She wanted to know if we had our fortunes told."

"Listen, I have to ask you a favor. Remember what you

told me about those kids buying stuff at your mother's store?" Martha prayed Phyllis wouldn't turn out to be a dud. She wasn't. She didn't miss a beat.

"The party for your sister, right?"

"Right."

"What about it? You haven't gone and told her, have you?"

"No, and that's the problem. A complication has developed." Martha took a quick peek through the crack in the closet door to make sure Jemima wasn't actually hovering. "She's taken a baby-sitting job," she whispered into the phone.

"On her birthday?"

"The same day. Can you phone Mrs. Bender? It's too dangerous to try it from here."

"You bet," said Phyllis conspiratorially.

"It's very important." Martha was still worried about trusting Phyllis to do the job.

"You can count on me," Phyllis said. "It's you who should be careful. Make sure you don't spill the beans."

"Of course I won't," Martha said hotly. Who was giving the orders, anyway? She felt like telling The Blot off but controlled herself. "Thanks a lot, Phyllis."

"You're welcome."

The closet door suddenly jerked open. Jemima was standing there. "Did the phone ring?" she asked.

"No!" Martha cried. "I mean, I'm talking to Teddy." She banged the phone down.

"I just thought maybe it rang," Jemima said dejectedly.

It was going to be hard not to tell. Martha forced

herself to remain strong. "It's early yet," she said. "It could ring anytime now that I'm off."

"Well, I don't care if it does or not!" Jemima shouted, and ran upstairs.

Martha vowed never to get involved with boyfriends if she could help it. A friend who was a boy was fine, but a boyfriend was a lot of trouble.

Martha went to find Mom to ask her about magazines. She had to get things ready for tomorrow. Mrs. Wish had given them a list of what she called her "curatives." Martha's job was to find pictures of places and things and the stages of life. Mrs. Wish suggested she cut the pictures out of magazines or books, but Martha would never cut up a book. It was lucky that Mom had a lot of old magazines in her nook, where she kept her home office.

"I was going to bring them to the recycling station," Mom said. "I'm glad I didn't." She smiled at Martha. "What kind of project is it you're doing for school?"

School, Martha thought. She had a bookbag full of homework!

"It's sort of a people project," Martha said.

"People are interesting, aren't they?" said Mom. "That's why I like my job so much. I never get tired of writing about people."

People might be interesting, Martha thought as she toiled up the stairs carrying an armload of magazines, but they sure did wear you out.

19.

After all her promises that she could be counted on, Phyllis was absent from school the next day. A million reasons ran through Martha's head. Maybe Phyllis caught a cold going all the way to Pineapple Street, or maybe her mother punished her for being late for dinner, or maybe she found out about the ghost. Worst of all, maybe Phyllis never did call Mrs. Bender and now what?

Martha couldn't concentrate on what Mrs. Ellery was saying. Teddy didn't make it any easier. He was as jumpy as a flea. At lunchtime he had no appetite for his peanut-butter-and-banana sandwiches.

Martha asked him if he'd managed to collect all the "curatives" on his list for Mrs. Wish.

"I got everything," Teddy said, looking miserable.

"I'm sure we have nothing to worry about," Martha said comfortingly. "Mrs. Wish will know how to get rid of the ghost."

"Oh, I don't care about some stupid old ghost! It's Buster I'm worried about."

"Buster will be fine too. Mrs. Wish loves him. Didn't you notice how she almost cried? She promised never to let him out without his tags again. And anyway, she's going to tie him up from now on."

"But that's just it! Maybe Buster doesn't want to go back now that he's had a taste of freedom. And I'm sure he won't like being tied up. Would you?"

Martha had a vision of herself tied up on a leash in her backyard and she couldn't help a giggle.

Teddy stared at her. "You're coldhearted, Martha. I wonder why I never noticed it before."

Martha bristled. "If there's anything I'm not, it's coldhearted. I got an F on my homework this morning, in case you didn't notice. I was too busy cutting up magazines instead of doing my assignment last night. All I do these days is things for other people. I never spend a minute thinking about myself!"

Now Teddy giggled. "You sound just like my mother when she gets on a kick."

Martha laughed with him.

"What do you think happened to Phyllis?" he asked. "We need her this afternoon. She's supposed to be bringing the candles."

"I hope we can trust that Blot."

"I thought she was pretty nice myself," Ted said.

"Oh, yeah?"

"I mean, she was a good sport about our scaring her and she's been very helpful."

"Especially when she buys us soda and ice cream," Martha declared.

Martha felt a queer twinge in her chest, near her heart. Probably heartburn, she thought, from the extra bean sprouts Mom had put on her sandwich. Maybe if she burped, she'd feel better.

"Phyllis is unreliable," she told Teddy, expecting him to agree.

"That's yet to be proved," Teddy said in a horribly reasonable way.

"My mom has some candles we can use," Martha said.

"Mrs. Wish wanted blue candles. I bet it's hard to find blue candles."

Martha felt mad and she didn't know why. She wasn't mad because Phyllis wasn't in school or because they might not have the blue candles for Mrs. Wish. It was some other kind of mad that made her feel all wishy-washy inside, like she was slopping around in melted butter.

"Why should a ghost care what color the candles are?" she snapped, and began clearing up her place.

Teddy didn't say anything. He gazed at Martha with a puzzled expression on his face. He mushed his glasses up and down his nose a few times. Then he suddenly got his appetite back and ate his two sandwiches in two gulps.

"I'm glad you recovered," Martha said watching him. "I was getting worried."

"I know," Teddy said. "Listen . . . Marth . . . I . . ." Suddenly he went all red in the face and quickly began gargling his milk out of the container.

He's the one who should have heartburn, Martha thought, amazed at his performance.

"I have to go to the library," she said. "Mrs. Ellery is making me do my homework before lunch is over."

"Okay. But . . . well . . . I just wanted to tell you . . ." Teddy suddenly gave a huge belch. "Sorry."

Martha waited, but he wiped his mouth on a napkin and stared into space.

"What?" she asked.

"What what?" he said.

"You wanted to tell me something."

"Oh, that. Yes. I wanted to say that you don't have to worry about Phyllis." He saw the impatient look on Martha's face and hurried on, the words coming out in a jumble. "I like you a lot better than I like her."

Martha gaped and then gathered up her things and ran out of the lunchroom. She felt embarrassed. She also felt better. The heartburn was gone and nothing seemed so bad anymore. In fact, everything seemed wonderful. She skipped down the hall to the library. She sort of blew in the door, practically humming.

"Well, Martha," said Mr. Pumphrey, the school librarian. "You certainly look happy today."

Martha stopped cold. In one awful brain-shattering moment she realized she was acting exactly like Jemima.

20.

Easy as pie, Mrs. Wish said it would be, when she arrived at the Rose house that afternoon. As soon as she got out of the taxi, her bracelets clanking and her red fingernails gleaming in the sun, she said the house had a nice atmosphere.

"Not at all morbid, that's a good sign," she said as the taxi driver assisted her up the path.

Martha and Teddy had been waiting, each with the "curatives" Mrs. Wish had ordered. In the shopping bag stuffed with magazine clippings were two tall white candles that Martha had snitched from the dining room. Her mom used them when she had special company for dinner. She hoped they'd be okay, even though they were the wrong color and had been burned down a little. Mrs. Wish had specifically asked for new blue candles.

At the last moment, when they were about to go inside the house, Phyllis came rushing down the street.

"I brought them," she puffed, holding up two blue candles wrapped in cellophane.

"Where were you, anyway?" Martha asked.

"Getting the candles, of course," Phyllis replied. "It wasn't easy. They didn't have any blue ones in town or in the mall. My mother took me to Southport."

"You skipped school to buy candles?" Teddy asked, awed.

Phyllis tossed her head and batted her eyelashes at him. "Sure, why not? You can trust me."

Martha didn't trust her. "But did you phone Mrs. Bender?" she asked, grabbing Phyllis's fluttering arm.

"Of course. And guess what? Mrs. Bender is in on the whole thing. That's why she asked your sister to baby-sit on her birthday. The party is going to be at the Benders' house. Isn't that great?"

"It'll be a great party, all right," said Teddy, adding some caustic remarks about Harvey Bender that nobody heard because a great woofing had begun inside the Rose house.

"Rocky!" Mrs. Wish cried, and hurried them along. "He knows I'm here!"

"He always barks when he hears us," Teddy said.

But once the door was opened, it was obvious. Martha had never seen such a display of whines and licks and rolling over on the floor, and wagging the nonexistent tail, and slobbering all over Mrs. Wish's black shoes and stockings. She and Teddy had never got a greeting like that.

Mrs. Wish went down creakily on one knee to give the dog a hug. The dog purred low in his throat and licked Mrs. Wish's ear.

"I guess there's no doubt about it," Teddy said, defeated at last.

As if feeling a little ashamed, Rocky extricated himself from Mrs. Wish's embrace and came over to jump on Teddy too. Martha helped Mrs. Wish get up. The bones in her knees snapped something awful.

"Well, let's get to work, shall we?" Mrs. Wish said, rubbing her hands.

They each had a special job. First Teddy was to go into the kitchen and heat up the cinnamon sticks, cloves, and spices he had brought in a big pot of water.

"A ghost likes a nice scent in the air," said Mrs. Wish, "contrary to what people think about damp cellars and musty attics."

Next, Phyllis set up the candles in the two candlesticks Mrs. Wish had brought. These were to be placed in the living room.

"Blue is a calm color," Mrs. Wish said. "It creates gentleness, and the flickering light of the candles softens the heart."

Finally, Martha had to set out the magazine pictures, in neat rows, on the living-room floor.

"This is most important," Mrs. Wish explained. "It's our only means of communication. It's hard to know the language of a ghost."

When all this was done, Mrs. Wish looked around, sniffed the cinnamony air, and told Rocky to sit quietly in a corner.

"Now," she said.

They gathered in a circle, bringing chairs together from other parts of the room. Mrs. Wish sat down and put her hands in her lap. The red fingernails looked like ten little ladybugs walking across her knees. She instructed them to be very quiet. Rocky shifted position, going around and around for a moment as dogs do. Mrs. Wish gave him a look and he stopped immediately. He lay back down with one last sigh.

There was silence. From far away Martha could hear

the faint sounds of a siren. That was all. Even their breathing seemed to have stopped.

Mrs. Wish was sitting up, straight and proper, in her chair. There was no sign of the ghost. Martha wondered if it would even bother to appear if they just kept sitting like bumps on a log. They'd made a lot of noise before and the ghost hadn't minded a bit. She was dying to call out to it.

She glanced over at Teddy and saw he was having a lot of trouble sitting still. Teddy always had to fidget. Phyllis was trying to look bored, but Martha knew she was covering up being scared.

Suddenly, Mrs. Wish's quavery voice said, "Hello? Are you there?"

A soft breeze ruffled Martha's hair. It was there, all right.

"We come as friends," Mrs. Wish went on. "We want to help you."

The harp gave a loud twang and Mrs. Wish jumped.

"Do you want to tell us something?" Mrs. Wish asked.

Of course it does, Martha thought impatiently. The harp strings pinged back in answer. The ghost seemed more polite than before, as if it was a little unsure of Mrs. Wish.

"Whatever you have to say, we'll listen," Mrs. Wish told it.

The harp began to play a little tune. It sounded sweet and sad at the same time. It reminded Martha of deep blue skies and the way the ocean looked after a long day at the beach, the waves gentle and golden with the setting sun. She could have listened to the music for a long time, but it ended too soon.

The ghost was sad, Martha realized. It had sung them a song of long ago, when it had been a real person and not yet a ghost.

"Thank you," Mrs. Wish said when the music stopped. "That was beautiful. Please tell us more. You may use the pictures we have provided."

The breeze moved across the floor, fluttering the magazine clippings. "That's right," Mrs. Wish said. "We'll ask you some questions and you can show us the answers."

"Now, children," she said, looking at them. "We need to find out why the ghost is here. Consider your questions carefully. We don't want to upset the creature."

Martha, Teddy, and Phyllis looked at each other. What kind of questions did you ask a ghost? In the library book Martha and Ted had read, it said most ghosts hung around because they had unfinished business. Martha knew that didn't mean the kind of business her dad left unfinished, like letters he had to write, or phone calls to make. A ghost's unfinished business probably had to do with something sad that had happened.

While Martha was trying to think how the ghost could tell about itself with only some old magazine pictures, Teddy asked the first and practical question.

"Who are you?"

The magazine pictures rustled and one of them floated upward toward Teddy. He shrunk back from it for a moment, then shrugged and reached out to catch it. "It's a picture of a girl," he said, turning it around so they could all see. It was a picture Martha had clipped from one of Jemima's old teenager magazines. The girl looked a little like Jemima, with frizzed-out hair and big eyes decorated with eyeshadow.

"So you're a teenager, huh?" Teddy said. "Hey!" The picture suddenly jumped out of Teddy's hand and went twirling through the air toward Mrs. Wish.

"A young girl," Mrs. Wish said. "But from long, long ago. I think that's what she's trying to tell us."

The harp pinged and they all knew the ghost had said yes.

"Well, what do we ask now?" Teddy questioned.

"Something happened, didn't it?" Martha said. "Right in this house, probably. And you're real sad about it, aren't you? I know you couldn't be happy, because then you wouldn't be hanging around. And you wouldn't have played that sad song on the harp."

The picture of the frizzed-out teenager landed in Martha's lap and slowly curled up into a ball.

Mrs. Wish's dark eyes were glittery with excitement. "We're certainly getting somewhere," she said. "Go on, Martha. I think you've established rapport."

Martha hoped rapport was good, whatever it was. She cleared her throat, and tried to think what to ask next. It was hard to think. And then she had a great idea. If this ghost was a long-ago teenager and something sad had happened, there was a good chance it wasn't too different from the sad things that happened now. Like Jemima thinking Denise was stealing Mellow away from her when they were only planning a surprise party. Probably the ghost was just like Jemima, a victim of misunderstanding.

"Did you have problems with your boyfriend?" Martha asked. "Maybe you didn't call them boyfriends way back then, but what I mean is, did you think he didn't love you anymore?"

Another magazine picture whirled into the air, fluttered across the room, and hovered in front of Martha's eyes. It was an advertisement for toothpaste. It showed a boy and girl smiling at each other. They looked like they each had at least a million blinding white teeth stuffed in their mouths. In the background was another girl, not smiling. She looked sorry she hadn't used the toothpaste. If she had, she wouldn't have lost her boyfriend.

Martha reached out to pluck the picture from the air. She showed it to the rest of them. Phyllis squinted. "Maybe the ghost has a toothache?" she asked. Martha gave her a disgusted look.

"You're waiting for him to come back, aren't you?" Martha asked the ghost. "You think you have to hang around just in case."

The harp pinged. Rocky looked up, ready to bark, but he caught Mrs. Wish's eye and stopped.

"You did great, Marth," Teddy said. "But now what can we do?" He looked at Mrs. Wish. "Do we have to try to find him? The boyfriend ghost?"

"I've got to be home for supper," Phyllis said. "My mom made me promise because of yesterday."

"Let me think," said Mrs. Wish.

"We only have until Sunday," Teddy said. "That's the deadline."

They all started talking about it, but Martha didn't join in. She sat in her chair, quietly thinking. She felt the ghost was sitting beside her, waiting for her solution.

"Wait a minute!" Martha exclaimed. They stopped talking and looked at her. "We don't have to find anyone.

We couldn't find the boy, anyway, because we have no way of knowing where he is. But a ghost could find another ghost. If our ghost would leave this house, she could go out and find her long-lost-love ghost and when she found him, everything would be all right."

The air danced next to Martha's chair, as if the ghost was jumping up and down with excitement.

"How do we know it will be all right?" Teddy asked doubtfully.

"Because it's all a misunderstanding. Just like my sister Jemima thinking Mellow didn't love her." And slowly and carefully, Martha explained to the ghost just what had happened, how Jemima had pined away for the last week and had finally given up.

"Next week, she'll see how wrong she was," Martha said. "But right now the misunderstanding seems very real."

"So if you go out and find your boyfriend," Teddy said, raising his voice to address the ghost, "you'll find out it was only a misunderstanding too."

"These guys are right," Phyllis contributed. "And it's almost time for supper."

"Martha's suggestion seems perfectly sound," said Mrs. Wish to the living-room air. "Now you tell us, dear, what do you think?"

For a moment there was no answer and they waited on tenterhooks. And then the harp began a lively jig, full of happiness and delight. It made them all feel like dancing. They shouted hooray and jumped around, even Mrs. Wish did, thumping her cane on the floor in time with the music. Rocky danced best though, leaping and cavorting and piercing the air with sharp barks.

And then, when the music stopped, the ghost took one last spin around the room, sending all the magazine clippings up into the air. With a great whoosh the ghost left the house. The front door slammed. It was gone. The magazine pictures came falling down on their heads, like confetti after a parade.

"Done!" exclaimed Mrs. Wish.

"Phew," said Teddy.

"Double phew," said Martha.

"You were wonderful," Mrs. Wish congratulated her. "I think the problem is solved and our ghost will live happily ever after in some other place."

"I'm sure glad it's over," Phyllis said, looking a little shaky. "I'm not used to these things."

"If you hang around with us, you'll have to get used to it," Martha advised.

"Yeah, we seem to get involved with a lot of this kind of thing," said Teddy.

"I was hoping you guys would let me hang around. Be friends with you, I mean," Phyllis said, grinning.

"Of course," Teddy said expansively. "How could we refuse someone who actually cut school to help us?"

Phyllis stopped grinning. She looked down at the floor and shuffled her feet. "Listen. Well. I—I have to tell you something. I didn't cut school to get the candles. The truth is I had an orthodontist appointment." Then she smiled again. "He's going to get rid of my vampire teeth."

"I've got to be going," Mrs. Wish said. Teddy, who had been laughing about Phyllis's vampire teeth, suddenly clamped his mouth shut.

"I'll be taking Rocky with me, Ted," Mrs. Wish said

gently. "But I want to discuss something with you first. Would you be willing to come over from time to time, to take Rocky for a walk and help me look after him?"

Teddy's face brightened. "Sure I would!"

"We'll settle the details later, but for now, it's a deal?" She put out her hand. Teddy took it and shook it, making sure he didn't get caught on the red fingernails. "Deal," he said.

Martha happily collected up all the magazine pictures and blew out the candles. Teddy and she washed out the pot of boiling cinnamon-and-spice water and turned out the lights. They locked the door behind them and waved to Mrs. Wish and Rocky getting into the taxi.

"All's well that ends well . . . again," said Teddy to Martha.

"Maybe for you guys," said Phyllis. "But my mother's gonna kill me. I'm ten minutes late for supper." She ran off down the street.

Teddy watched her, shaking his head. "You wouldn't think there would be so much fuss about a dinner that's made in the microwave."

21.

The Roses returned to the house next door.

Martha ran right over to give them the twenty dollars back. Mrs. Wish had reimbursed them for the money she and Ted spent on dog food and chewy bones.

"The ghost is gone," she assured them.

They seemed pleased, but Mr. Rose said they would spend the night to see for sure. And the next morning they were outside at seven A.M., making a lot of noise, annoying Dad and shouting to Martha that the house was no longer haunted. Luckily, Mom didn't catch on and think Martha had anything to do with it.

Instead, she shook her head and laughed. "I guess we're stuck with them," she said. "But at least they got rid of their silly ideas. As if a dull old house like that could be haunted!"

Martha felt relieved. For the first time in a week she had been able to do her homework. It was going to take some hard work to make up for all the F's. But she still had one small problem left. Jemima. She wasn't sure Jemima would survive the week. If only this one final problem would get solved, Martha thought, she would promise to get nothing but A's.

She didn't have much hope, though. And then, like a miracle, Jemima's mood changed.

"How come you're so happy all of a sudden?" Martha asked, horribly worried that Jemima had found a new boyfriend.

Jemima jumped around like a nut and gave Martha a rare hug. "I'm so happeeee!" she screeched. "Can you keep a secret?"

Don't ask, Martha thought, but she nodded.

"I was wrong. Denise doesn't want Mellow. They're giving me a surprise party!" She jumped around some more and then sobered up and began yanking at the waistband of her jeans. "Now I really have to go on a diet! Those creeps. They could have told me!"

"But then it wouldn't have been a surprise," Martha said reasonably. "How did you find out?"

"Harvey told me."

Typical, Martha thought. "Great," she said, "now the surprise is spoiled."

"No, it isn't," Jemima said. "I can still act surprised. I'll make it look good. But at least I'll be wearing the right clothes."

"What if Harvey lets on you know?"

"He won't! I threatened to throw his snotty stuffed pig in the garbage if he breathes a word!"

Jemima went jumping off like a gazelle. Martha stood on the sidewalk in front of the Rose house, watching her go. That's that, she thought. My wish came true and now I have to do homework like crazy so I can get all A's. Well, it was worth it. All the problems have been solved and there's nothing else that can go wrong.

At that moment a taxi pulled up in front of the Rose

house. A tall, skinny woman got out. Martha looked and then had to look again.

Of all people, it was Miss Hatton, the teacher they hated most. She stomped up the path, her sharp nose darting everywhere. Martha tried to slink behind a bush, but Miss Hatton saw her and pounced.

"Martha Lewis!" she said. "What are you doing here?"

Martha felt trapped and had to remind herself she didn't need to make excuses for standing in her own front yard. "I live here."

Miss Hatton's face broke into a skeleton smile. "How nice," she shouted. "We'll be seeing a lot of each other from now on!"

Martha tried to arrange her face so that Miss Hatton couldn't tell what she was thinking. But Miss Hatton's sharp nose had a way of smelling everything out.

She pointed to the Rose house. "Have you met my sister? Mrs. Flora Rose?" she asked.

Appalled, Martha nodded.

"She's giving me music lessons," Miss Hatton said, and walked briskly up the porch steps and rapped on the Rose front door.

Martha couldn't believe it. But it was true. After a few moments a sound of music drifted out. Clangy and twangy, worse than anything ever played by an angry ghost, came the sound of Miss Hatton playing the harp.